PENGUIN BOOKS
MOMENTS OF DESIRE

Susan Hawthorne works as an editor and reviewer. She has been actively involved in the Women's Liberation Movement for more than fifteen years. She has worked in a variety of jobs including teaching at universities, as a youth worker, a teacher of English as a second language and as an organiser of writers' festivals.

She is the editor of *Difference: Writings by Women*, and her stories, poems, articles and reviews have been published widely in Australia and overseas. She is working on a collection of stories and a novel.

Jenny Pausacker first combined feminism and writing in the Women's Liberation Children's Literature Co-operative, and she has since worked on plays with the Adelaide Women's Theatre Group, as well as various equal opportunity resources. She holds a PhD in children's literature but writes for all age groups. Basically she prefers the novel and has had seven children's novels published. Her novel, *What Are Ya?* was shortlisted for the 1988 Victorian Premier's Award for Children's Literature.

Other books by these authors

Susan Hawthorne
Difference: Writings by Women (editor)

Jenny Pausacker
What Are Ya? (teenage fiction)
Can You Keep a Secret? (children's fiction)

MOMENTS OF DESIRE

Sex and Sensuality by Australian Feminist Writers

Edited by
Susan Hawthorne
and Jenny Pausacker

Penguin Books
Assisted by the Literature Board of the Australia Council

Penguin Books Australia Ltd
487 Maroondah Highway, PO Box 257
Ringwood, Victoria, 3134, Australia
Penguin Books Ltd
Harmondsworth, Middlesex, England
Viking Penguin Inc.
40 West 23rd Street, New York, NY 10010, USA
Penguin Books Canada Limited
2801 John Street, Markham, Ontario, Canada, L3R 1B4
Penguin Books (N.Z.) Ltd
182–190 Wairau Road, Auckland 10, New Zealand

First published by Penguin Books Australia, 1989

Typeset in 10/11pt Bembo by Renwick Pride Pty Ltd Albury NSW
Made and printed in Australia by Australian Print Group, Maryborough, Victoria

CIP

Moments of Desire.

ISBN 0 14 012303 2.

1. Women — Literacy collections.   2. Feminism, Literary collections.   3. Women
— Sexual behavior — Literary collections.   4. Literature — Women authors.   5.
Sex in literature.   I. Hawthorne, Susan.   II. Pausacker, Jenny.   III. Australia
Council. Literature Board.

808.89'9287

Creative Writing Program assisted by the Literature Board of the Australia Council,
the Federal Government's arts funding and advisory body.

Some say an army on horseback,
some an army on foot,
still others say a fleet of ships remains
the most beautiful sight in
this dark world;
but I say it is
whatever you desire.

Sappho

Editors' Acknowledgements

We would like to thank the contributors for their patience in the putting together of this anthology. Jane Arms' editorial eye has been invaluable. Thanks also go to Kaye Moseley for her support; to Jackie Yowell for her faith in the project; to Susanne von Paczensky for her critical response; to Nancy Peck and Renate Klein for their ongoing critical comments and support; and to Bruce Sims and others at Penguin who turned the idea into a reality. Finally, we would like to thank one another as co-editors, although, over the four years of working together, we have not always agreed, our discussions have always helped us to clarify our ideas.

Contents

INTRODUCTION

Several years ago we decided to edit an anthology of feminist erotica. It proved to be a longer job than we had anticipated, and in the process we read a lot of creative writing about sex, discussed the issues with a variety of people, examined a wide range of articles on the feminist debate about erotica and pornography, and we changed our determining premises several times.

One of the reasons for our shift is the complexity of issues surrounding the depiction of women's sexuality. The dividing line between erotica and pornography is a blurred one. The new category of non-violent erotica proposed by the Australian government is a good example: the exclusion of violence is no guarantee that concepts of submission and dominance will be excluded. We knew that we were looking for writing that did not use the structural power differences between women and men as the basis for eroticisation, and the immediate problem we faced was one of language. Pornography, with its close associations with a male-dominated sex industry, seemed inappropriate as a description for feminist writing about sex. In contrast, erotica appeared to allow more space for the desires and needs of women, although we did sometimes wonder whether, in historical terms, erotica was not simply upper-class pornography.

Then, inevitably, we were faced with the question of whether particular stories and poems were or were not erotic. When we talked with our friends we found that a single piece could have one person declaring, 'That's the most erotic thing I've ever read,' and yet leave another reader unmoved. What was more confusing, we knew from the start that we wanted to include pieces that dealt with the difficulties, hesitations and complications surrounding sex, but we worried that no one else would consider it erotic . . .

We reacted, then, against the notion of a guaranteed 'turn-on' that seemed to be implicit in all the definitions. We remembered, with relief, that we had begun working on the anthology because we wanted to see a greater variety of writing about sex, so that the diversity of women's experiences would have a greater chance of being represented. We were not obliged to present our readers with the definitive 'feminist erotic experience': the very idea was a contradiction in terms. We changed our sub-title once more, and at last it seemed to fit the anthology.

Some readers may question the inclusion of stories and poems about exchanging a look, eating a meal, or turning forty, but as we see it, all these pieces are about sexual feelings, whether or not they are about sexual acts. We realised that the power of some of the pieces lay not so much in *what* happened, but in *how* it happened, or what *might* have happened. So desire – even moments of it – became our integrating theme.

Moments of Desire also contains writing that is sexually explicit in a way that remains unusual for women writers, and such pieces raise different kinds of questions. The one thing we can say for sure is that there is no consensus among feminists who are writing about sex to establish that one word is too crude or that another is a euphemism. Women are still making exploratory choices about language: when to name and when to indicate, when to use colloquial terms and when to use image and metaphor; and this anthology contains many different choices.

Similarly, the voices heard here vary enormously. Some writers have chosen a poetic or experimental approach; others have opted for a traditional narrative structure. Our guiding principle, both in terms of style and content, was to range as widely as possible, from the sexual experiences of children or adolescents to the sexual feelings of old women; from writers who took on a male persona to writers who confronted the theory of the erotic head on; from eroticism of less than ecstatic sex to the dissatisfactions of ecstatic sex. As editors we also worked to represent a range of sexual alternatives – celibacy, lesbianism, heterosexuality, bisexuality – although we were surprised, and pleased, by the number of writers who showed no concern with pronouns or details of anatomy, concentrating instead on simple sensual awareness.

We do not see the range of the collection as definitive. There is little indication in this anthology, for example, of cultural differences in women's experiences of sex, but our hope is that *Moments of Desire* will prompt other writing and other anthologies. We do believe, however, that a collection of *feminist* writing about sex adds a political dimension to the debate about women's experiences of desire and pleasure. The writers in this book continue the feminist tradition of turning personal experiences into political action. Creative writing has a special part to play in developing a new language of sexuality.

Susan Hawthorne and Jenny Pausacker
February 1989

THE MAP OF THE WORLD

Anna Couani

The map of the world is felt from the inside. Rough around the coast-lines and smooth over the hills and sand dunes. Warm and moist through the rivers which lead outside to the forests like long hair then sparser like shorter more bristly hair to the touch. Reading a globe of the world with its topography in relief. Reading with the fingers as though blind. Feeling it with the back, down the spine. Making contact with the nipples and the nose only. Moving at a fast rate underwater through the oceans and large lakes. Most of the oceans connect up with each other. Moving so fast that you become aware of the earth's surface being curved. Flying low but fast across the land masses. Make yourself feel like the world. As old but not as troubled.

EROTICA ALPHABETICA

Susan Hawthorne

and as an arm
brushes breast   body
caressing
delightful desire
eros   erotica
fine feeling
glowing
handling her hair
in intimacy
je t'aime   I insist
kindled
love   licking lips   labia
majora   minora   mouth
nipple
opening   oh   oh
pleasure
quietly
rippling   rubbing
slippery surfaces
tongue tingling   tongue
ululating under
vulval
wetness
xx
you   your
zephyr zone

Use More Hooks

Marion Halligan

The women walking bare-breasted along the beach. Promenading. French promenading, not English. The pines above, the tufted palms rattling more noisily than the striped umbrellas in the lazy breeze, the idle café-tables inviting loungers. And watchers. And the women walking bare-breasted in the dull sunlight, their boobs pointing pert or tumbling and bumbling ahead of them. All ages, all sizes. It is impossible for foreign eyes to look at anything else, just these breasts coming towards you; not at faces or stomachs, except occasionally when the belly wobbles below like some enormous third boob, or when the breasts are so beautiful that you raise your eyes to the face above to see the graced possessor of such perfection.

But most of the women are simply thin, *mince* as can be, from guarding their lines all winter, with small decorous swellings decorating the flying buttresses of their rib cages. And so brown, so *bronzée*. She's read the magazines. You'd think from them that every woman in the country was basking herself, basting herself with rich unguents, to turn pale biscuit into toast into shining brazen image.
– He looks slyly sideways at her copious bikini.
– Wouldn't you like to join them? he says.
– No, she says. And besides I'd look stupid. I'd be wearing a white bikini top I can't take off.
– I'd love a sunburnt nipple, he says.
– Do they turn you on? she asks.
– Not *en masse*, he sighs.

Beyond is the sea, flat, slightly metallic, absurdly gentle. Only theoretically are people here to swim in it. It is a backdrop to the promenading; a rather dull backdrop.
– Not surprising, she says. A sea to swim in ought to be energetic.

She thinks of the wind and the salt and the noise of breakers that have rolled five thousand miles. But not nostalgically. She is here for the civilisation, after all, in seas as well as cities.

That evening they drive along the coast, tourists with their *Michelin Guide* seeking a restaurant worth a visit. Not a detour, not as superb and expensive as that, but worth a visit if passing. She orders *tellines* for first course, the slowest dish she's ever eaten. A myriad minute shellfish, each as large and pearly golden pink as the nail on her ring finger. Each has to be separately sucked for its tiny gobbet of flesh. And then the juice spooned up and mopped with bread. He, who has consumed his dish of *calmar* in a fraction of this time, gets drunk waiting for her to finish. Or is so by the time they have eaten their way through several more courses and returned to the hotel through the mother-of-pearl twilight. And he is ready to sleep. Falling snorting to the pillow in a heavy wine-slumber. Ignoring the fact that the moon is about to rise and doubtless make a silver pavement across the sea romantic beneath the windows.

She sleeps too, and dreams. Dreams herself bare-breasted and bounding through the sea, not the slatternly Mediterranean but the vigorous seas of home. She frolics, disports, cavorts. Gallops through the frothing shallows and dives into the waves that roll about her, bearing her up, tossing her down, energetically caressing. Her breasts are free, they bob in the waves; she is exhilarated. And when she wakes, the fine exhilaration of the dream remains with her.

– Probably the shellfish, he says from inside the cavern of his hangover.

Shellfish. Shells. And she Venus. Venus of the pearly golden pink shells, the myriad buoyant *tellines* floating her across the sea. Not the freshborn modest girl coyly draping her hair but a mature wanton woman disporting. She feels a dark excitement, as if adulterous.

They walk through the town, to the seafront, for breakfast. They stop at an *agence de presse* for postcards to send to the children, far away at home with Granny, and she buys a magazine. Her French is good enough to allow her to feel she is experiencing the country from inside by reading its popular literature. They sit on the terrace of the café. The waiter brings coffee and bread, with jam and butter in little dishes, not foil. It will cost a packet. The beach is empty: it's too early for the breasts. The sea is slightly misty, still flat. You'd say there wasn't enough buoyancy in it to support even an extra *mince* Venus on a shell. He reads an elderly English newspaper, checking up on how much closer the world is to perishing, or was the day before yesterday, and she looks at *Elle*. Reads the film reviews and the information on summer festivals, and then comes to the fashion section: underwear. At first sight a lot of girls disporting themselves on frothing beds. Slender, but not at all *bronzeé*. Peachy-pearly rather. And the garments are confections of satin and lace and complicated knottings of ribbons, handmade, of real silk, and costing far more than she'd expect to spend on clothing for the outside. One is even a corset, a delicate cage of whalebone bound in satin with a row of hooks down the back. Called a *guepière*: a wasp waister. '*The grand come-back of delicate lingerie*', says the headline. '*Nacrée ou saumonée, elle est douce, voluptueuse, seduisante*'. Soft, voluptuous, seductive. Sounds like a line from Baudelaire: *Luxe, calme, et voluptée*. Or something. Mother of pearly or salmon pink: sounds like last night's shellfish. And then because this is a French magazine and even seduction is to be intellectualised, it quotes from a leading sociologist: 'Women whom the sexual liberation has rendered easily denudable 'undressable?' are seized with regret for a time when the price of falling was measured by the number of hooks to undo.' And there is the means to recover all the old lost fun of seduction: a wasp-waisting hourglass of whalebone with a row of hooks down the back. And notice the word 'falling': a titillating sense of sin suggested. What luxury.

She laughs. Or sighs. Lifts her eyes to the beach. Still no brown women, of the ultimately easy denudability – the hooking of a finger in a pubic sliver of cloth will instantly reveal all – but a species of lifeguard, fiddling with deck chairs. His chest and arms a series of curved muscular planes, very *bronzé* too, anointed with oil and gleaming. The people at the café are his audience: his skin ripples with the consciousness of them. She remembers when feminism first became fashionable, and certain magazines for women presented pictures of naked men, standing round in forests, or lying on beaches, pricks cocked. Well, sometimes. Oddly enough, not really very exciting. Particularly since she prefers men like the thin clever-tongued one here beside her. And anyway she has a theory that women are turned on by images not of the opposite sex but of their own. She finds these pictures of half-clothed women on satiny beds provocative, but less from a desire to join than to emulate, to identify with that opulent flesh. Herself possessor of it as owner, not user. Vicarious mistress of desire. Wanton Venus, disporting in all the trimmings of luxury. A couch for luxury . . .

She is about to show the pictures to her husband dark-glassed against the misty morning glare, explain her theory, but he is pushing away coffee cups, folding up newpaper, urging on.

– We'd better get off. A lot to do today. A long drive ahead.

She puts the magazine away. The breakfast of tourists is not a good time for initiating the complicated processes of seduction.

BUTTERFLY

Barbara Hanrahan

I used to get hysterical about not having a penis. They had a penis and I didn't. I didn't have anything – I was a nothing. I had nothing and they had something. My brother stood up and peed in the bath.

Dad had a giant's penis. Dad got cross because I worried that I didn't have a penis. Dad told me how he'd been a little girl and somehow he became a man, but he didn't explain it very well. Mum said when she'd wanted a baby she'd found me in a strawberry patch. There were strawberries down the bottom of our backyard and I couldn't stop eating them. There was a strawberry on the end of Dad's penis. I had a dream that I sat in the strawberry patch and stuffed strawberries up my butterfly so I'd grow a penis. Mine was a butterfly because it had pink wings that opened – a butterfly with that pink bit down the middle.

Sometimes I'd go off with some girls and we'd get other kids' little brothers. They were so little they had to do everything we said. We'd pull their pants down and have a good look.

My cousin Henry made me look at his penis and it had a pinker strawberry than Dad's. He showed me how to make it stand up. He held his penis and rubbed it up and down and then it got really stiff and stood poking at me like somebody's finger telling you off. Henry's mother had died, and he lived with Grandma. She had a floral carpet and he'd stand there peeing all over it, saying he was watering the flowers. Grandma's carpet stank of pee. Grandma said Henry's mother, Aunt Ruth, had hated her big mammary glands so she went on to slimming pills and got addicted and starved herself to death.

When my brother played with his penis, Mum said she'd take him to the hospital to have it cut off. I thought I could have his penis stitched on to me. Because I wanted to have a penis, Mum said she'd take me to England. There was a special hospital in England where they turned girls into boys.

I got hysterical because they wouldn't let me play football or sell newspapers. There were a lot of things they wouldn't let me do because I wasn't a boy. When I had a dress on, I couldn't climb trees, because I'd show my pants. When I went hysterical, I'd bang my head against the wall. Then I'd be so tired I'd just lie on the bed and pick at the wall, and all the little marks became like birds in the sky.

It was all right to see Dad and my brother without clothes on, but you weren't allowed to be curious. My brother and I used to have a bath together. He'd have the good end and I'd have the plug end with the taps in my back. Once my brother made me sit on the lavatory, and then he peed between my legs.

When Grandpa lay on the beach in his pyjama kind of shorts I looked up the leg and saw a big slug hanging out: Grandpa had a sort of big white slug glued to the side of his leg.

I'd look at men's pants to see if their penis hung on the left or the right side. If they were left-handed their penis was usually on the right side; if they were right-handed they put it away on the left. If you had a penis, you had to flick it to knock the drops off after you'd peed. Dad told my brother to do that.

Once I was in Dad's shed watching him working on the car. And I wanted to go to the lavatory, but I wanted to watch him, and I waited one more minute, and then it came out in my pants. It was hanging there like in a sling, and Dad had to take me inside and empty it out.

I was always making lavatories. I'd dig a hole by the strawberry patch and put grass in it. Then I'd pull my pants down and sit in the hole. I liked the soft feeling of the grass.

They started building houses in the paddocks behind our back-yard. I'd hold myself in all day, and when the builders went home I'd take some lavatory paper into a house and do it in the big pipe where the lavatory was going to be. But Mum caught me and hit me. She said I was dirty-minded. She was always cleaning me out with Laxettes and worm pills and Velvet soap – Mum would cut off a bit of soap and grab me and jam it up my bottom.

Melva Button lived next door. She had a false tooth and was sort of rabbit looking. And she had a turned-up nose, like it was pushed against a window. The Buttons were Church of Christ and Mr Button used Tally-Ho cigarette papers, but Dad didn't smoke. Melva had Rock Hudson pinned on her bedroom wall, and the Buttons had lots of Pat Boone records. Mr Button had a new FJ Holden and a motorbike with a sidecar and a leather jacket he'd got in the war. He could whistle in perfect tune and kept *Man* magazines in the kitchen drawer next to the knives and forks. When you looked at a *Man* magazine, a feeling came in your butterfly, but if you heard Mr Button coming you'd slam it back in the drawer. Melva said the ones that looked naked weren't, because they wore flesh-coloured tights. Melva and I put our mothers' brassières on and then filled them up with socks to see whose were the biggest. Mrs Button worked at Mylady's Dainties, so Melva had pants with lace and satin bows, but Mum made mine from old flannel sheets. When Mum gave me a gold locket with a bluebird on it, Melva's mother gave her a bigger one with a photo of Melva inside.

Sometimes I went to the beach with the Buttons, but Melva always saw sharks where I was swimming; and we'd go into the ladies' changing rooms to look at their bottoms when they were undressing and their fronts when they came out of the showers. When it was the caterpillar plague, Melva squashed them and collected their green insides in jars. Melva liked to shut me in rooms and pretend she'd turned the gas on so I'd die, and I'd lie there dying. Melva showed me how filmstars did tongue kissing, but I didn't like the taste of her spit. Melva would fill up a lemonade bottle with water and drink it, then see if she could pee as much as she'd drunk. Melva said how when you were grown up blood came out of your butterfly. I didn't believe it, and when I asked Mum she hit me with the electric jug cord.

Melva made me play Dirty Doctors. Usually we played Dirty Doctors in Melva's playhouse, but sometimes we played it inside Melva's wardrobe with a torch. I was always the patient and Melva would say I looked dreadfully sick and give me injections with Mrs Button's sewing needles and then I'd have to take my pants off.

Melva was Church of Christ and I was Methodist, but Jesus was treated better in the Catholic church round the corner, where they had pictures and statues of Him everywhere. I'd try to make friends with Catholic girls so I could go into their bedrooms to see their statues, and I'd stare at Jesus so hard He'd talk to me. One girl had a crucifix with a hole you looked through to read the Lord's Prayer. I'd lie in the strawberry patch and see the angels coming through the clouds.

The date palms in the park were like big pineapples stuck in the ground. On Palm Sunday we cut palm fronds off and took them to Sunday School. Somebody was Jesus and somebody was the donkey and He rode under our arch of palm fronds. On the way home from Sunday School we danced round and pretended our palm fronds were grass skirts.

Once after Palm Sunday, Melva and I were in the playhouse playing Dirty Doctors. Melva made me lie down and started giving me injections with a palm-frond needle to make me go to sleep. Then she got lots of little stones and put them in my butterfly.

I called it my butterfly, but Mum called it your private. Sometimes I'd see PRIVATE on a door.

MAGILL ROAD

Rosemary Jones

We lived upstairs, above a Coca-Cola sign.
We lived upstairs in a bed-sit, she and I.
We lived like aristocracy.

We ate brie and caviar and dolmades. We ate ham from the bone with strong mustard. We ate baklava. We grew parsley and basil in a window-box above the Coca-Cola sign.

We looked down on the street. Things happened in the street. Cheek to cheek, eyeball to eyeball. Sometimes we hung ourselves over the Coca-Cola sign; we draped ourselves over it on warm summer evenings as if we were in a circus.

It was a circus at our place. A circus of expressions. Gestures. Mimicry. Dance. Song. Clown acts.

We were very happy. We were especially happy some nights. We would drink a lot and dangle from the Coca-Cola sign, giggling and waving to passing motorists. Or young punks with orange hair. Or grandmothers. That made us happy.

We would laugh because in the morning we would count the bottles, then spread them up the street, sharing them out evenly among the neighbours' rubbish.

And they were not bottles of Coca-Cola.

They were rieslings, chardonnays, champagnes.

Quite a lot of champagne. I told you, we lived like aristocracy.

We did not pay much rent. So we lived it up. We lived like royalty above the Coca-Cola sign. Which flashed. Intermittently, as we lay in bed. In the bed-sit. In the one huge white-walled room with the toilet to one side.

We laughed a lot in the bed-sit and watched as the sign flashed, on-off-on.

'You've got a flasher,' someone said.

'That is a very clichéd joke,' we said. 'What's more it is unoriginal.'

They thought they were being clever. We were tired of people being clever. We thought we were being adventurous instead, when we crawled out to the flashing sign and sat astride it, drinking straight from a bottle of French champagne.

We were in the money then. What we saved on rent we spent on food.

Once, under a full moon, we sat astride the flashing red and white Coca-Cola sign.

Downstairs, someone called the police.

We overheard them. Their outraged voices floated through the still night air and up to us.

By the time they came, we were sound asleep in the huge bed next to the window-ledge. It was getting too cold out there, anyway. The police woke us up.

'Police here,' they said.

'What?' we said to each other, looking askance.

'Police here. Open up!'

We scurried down to meet them in our nighties. They were new nighties too. What we saved on rent we spent on nighties, with lace.

'What's the matter?' We peered at them. 'Is something wrong?' We looked concerned.

They were fresh-faced and pink-cheeked. We chatted them up.

'Sorry to disturb you ma'am,' they said twice, once to each of us.

'I should think so,' we said.

We crawled back up the stairs and made love very close to the window-ledge but not on the Coca-Cola sign. Someone might have dobbed us in again.

'Perhaps it would be good for the deli's business,' we said, 'to do it on the sign.'

We contemplated turning the first C into a ♀ but by that time the landlord was getting suspicious. He loved Coca-Cola.

He didn't like us. We dressed in too many colours, like clowns. We had too many books, suspiciously titled. And apart from that we lived in a bed-sit with only one bed.

If we were sisters it might have been okay to sleep in the bed together. We weren't sisters. And what's more we hated Coca-Cola.

We hung out our washing on the sign. Knickers and things. That made the landlord really suspicious.

'Bet he's a perve,' someone said.

'Typical,' someone said.

'Give him a run for his money,' someone said.

Every day we put knickers on the Coca-Cola sign. We hung them out to dry.

He got very red in the face. Flabbergasted and flustered. We loved it. We thrived on it.

We washed out knickers even before they needed washing and hung them out to dry on the Coca-Cola sign.

We thought we might lose our bond money. Until we realised we hadn't paid a bond. He was into tax lurks. So we put out our brassières. A final gesture. We rustled them up from the bottom of our drawers and hung them out.

The landlord went redder in the face. We giggled. We were good at giggling, especially in the middle of the night. We usually drank champagne then.

When he threw us out in an apoplexy of rage we laughed. And left our stockings strangling the Cs of the Coca-Cola sign. Not to mention bottles of scent and empty talc containers in the bathroom, and a lip-sticked sign cheekily scrawled on the mirror.

You can make that bit up if you like.

You can make up the end of the story.

But I should tell you we moved to Sydney and lived in Balmain, where there was a distinct shortage of Coca-Cola signs.

And we had to make love, inside.

Beverley Farmer

A bubble of milk
will ooze out of the taut stem
when you pick a fig —
don't drink, the milk tastes bitter
though it looks like a man's juice.

When ripe to bursting
figs pass a drop of syrup
that glows at their pink
puckered holes. Put your mouth there.
Open the red seed-bellies.

The Last Pages of Ulysses

Finola Moorhead

for Kris

She is waiting for the man
who never comes
to the door

the man who doesn't exist
any more

and yet she waits
while her husband is away
during the day

her floors are clean
being cleaned
doing cleaning first
then recognising
thirst

defrosts the fridge
as she finds
as she takes out the soft drink
that it, the fridge,
needs to be done

the washing machine
whirs, gurgles, clunks
spins the clothes
then she is out
in the sun

still she is waiting

and she doesn't ring her lover
although she, the lover,
may come
to the door
come at her call

and come, most certainly,
with her touch

she sits down to a cup
of tea
takes a book on her knees

reads
the last pages of *Ulysses*
the rave of Molly Bloom
luxuriating in bed
dreaming of soldiers
taken by fever or war
with the Boers

she thinks perhaps
another rest
this time with coffee
and *The White Hotel*
upon her knee

she reads the poem
or rather begins
the beginning of the book

but restlessness
drags her from mirror
to mirror in the house
and guilt places a feather
duster in her left hand

the right combs back her hair
time and again
it's a strange day

untimely heat
and memories
of beaches,
bush creeks

and rivers
where love was made
in the past
sets her dreaming
of other lovers
other husbands

it is the heat

the ringing of cicadas
is missing

when the phone intrudes
it is her lover
whom she loves

but rejects
a visit now

somehow

returns to the poem
of luscious sex and fantasy

chides her own sincerity
yes insincere
a sham
a parasite

she must cook food
sometime
should she shop?

sex and love
seem separate suddenly

she'd like to read
some porn
written especially for her

but she waits

prepares cold tomatoes
for lunch
love-apples
belladonna
tomatoes full of seeds

and juice
she has no passionfruit
no mango
no paw paw, papaya

vague boredom
tension
tiredness
she looks
at the mirror door
of her pill cupboard
into her own eyes
which suggest

no

no to some pill-gotten high
she goes into her garden
the sun is hot
some of the washing's dry

she doesn't care
she squats on the lawn
to stare
at the flowers
butterflies
insect things
tries to guess the notes
and intervals
as a bird sings
doing nothing
and waiting
for nothing

except in a few moments
to crack the ice
and clean the fridge

she seems lazy

she checks the vegie
situation

the little eye
of a zucchini

like the top of a cock
catches her glance

why not
she needs
a chance
there's no one
around
no man who isn't a man
a person with demands

she grasps the vegetable
in her hand
closes around it

then mouths it
in and out

nothing but
curiosity,
imagination

she fixes the zucchini
in her pants
it is so like
a hard penis
she is surprised

it's beautiful
she feels it there
thrusting firmly
at her jeans

she takes herself
to the mirror in the bedroom
and looks at her ambiguous
crotch,
it is there, hard and soft

she rubs it with her fingers
and says aloud,
'no one need know'

with the vegetable there
she goes about her house–
work

the washing is dry
she takes it down from the line
and places it carefully
in the plastic basket
folding slowly

smiling a little
and touching the zucchini
in her trousers
quite often

her mind still curious
her body gently being

'i am alone,
but what's this guilt'

she attacks the fridge
cleaning fast
as if she has an appointment
at three in the afternoon

she doesn't dwell
on terms like 'dildo'
fingering it through the denim
it feels exactly right
like his was
once
dancing
as if it were alive
as if it were her own
sitting securely
beside her clitoris
her own parts
hugging it
keeping it erect

another husband
another lover
bush streams
mountain rivers
the beach too
all blessed
being done

being memories
or pictures of romance
the loved one
vague personless
either man or woman

having finished
the fridge
she stands
arms akimbo
and laughs
as if it were
one of those days
and the lover were there
to nibble the ear
to answer with giggles

but it's just
a zucchini
and a hot ordinary day
by herself with the housework

she thought she was normal
she is not perverse
even so
in her busy street
where pedestrians pass by
she goes out
to her mailbox
with the zucchini
like a penis in her jeans
and standing there
she reads her mail
scurries inside
'i am alone
why tease myself'

she sets the mirror
at the end of the bed
lies down
takes the wet and warm
zucchini in her hand

wonders what first to do

will her now tense and guilty
mind make trouble
and bring in ugly things

the zucchini reaches deep into her
and she makes it like a man
thrusting urgently
it's nice but not like the sex
she's known
the sensation is easy
all the time in the world

she takes it out and sucks
her juices from the vegetable
and sees in the mirror
that her cunt's alive

she does to herself
all the things she hopes
her man would do
but doesn't
it is different
she decides
then she becomes the woman
lover of herself
and finally she comes
leaving the wet zucchini
lying on her stomach

then
she
realises
she has betrayed

both lover and husband
because she is replete
she is now
inside her own day
and the birds sing
the traffic hums
and she feels sulky
beautiful and loved

she sleeps

when she wakes
she makes the bed
replaces the mirror
showers
the zucchini she puts aside
on her work bench
she feels alone
yet loved
by some invisible force

more work to do
she goes to the shops
in a post-coital state
and thinks of food

she meets her lover in the street
and invites her home for dinner

her husband, lover and herself
eat zucchini, stir fried vegetables
and meat

and she cannot say
what she has been doing
during the day

to murmur, 'just the usual'
seems a colossal lie

A LOVE STORY

Marian Eldridge

(1) Legend

When Philip wakes again it is daylight; as window, wash-basin, chair and then rucksacks swim into focus, this time he knows where he is: in a room in a pensione in Florence, just a stone's throw from the bridge where Dante saw Beatrice, exams over, his girl beside him. Three months of travelling. Seeing. Voyage to Discovery. New World finds Old. He turns his head; Alvie is still asleep. Sitting up carefully, he watches a pulse ticking in her neck. Her skin is pale, winter-pale, but across the pillow her hair is a copper fire. She has used the rinse she bought to try out her phrase-book Italian. Her lips move; she is smiling. At what, he wonders, sliding out of the bed. What?

Shivering in the cool of late autumn, he pulls on jeans and skivvy and, lifting the chair over to the window, opens his notebook. What he reads there doesn't seem too bad, quite good in fact. Before she wakes up he will have another go at it, see if this morning he can't pin down in verse all the dazzle of paint, the curve and gleam of marble that has made him feel drunk – stoned – feverish since he stepped off the plane back in Rome.

He glances across at Alvie; her eyelids flutter. Stay asleep, darling, he begs. Let me get this right first. Alvie is a bit terse sometimes about his notebook – a habit grown out of all that solitariness, a whole four-fifths of his life actually, so long he used to think being alone was fate's lot for him. She says it's an obsession, this need to get it right. Just dash off a few impressions, she says, the rest will come later, you know it will. Stop *worrying*, Phil. Relax. Take a deep breath. Take more photos – they'll bring it all back. Or postcards – buy postcards like me. And she flicks through things that have caught her eye: a fountain in Rome that they came upon unexpectedly at the end of a long day when they were on the edge of quarrelling; and that statue of the naked boy about to kiss his girl; nice that, she says, Love hugging his Psyche.

What she doesn't understand, broods Philip, hunched up under the window, is that it's not simply a matter of making notes of everything like some indiscriminate camera. No. That isn't bothering him. It's the shape within all the shapes and colours – *that's* what keeps eluding him.

He looks down at his notes. It's no good, the words won't move, they lie shrivelled and limp. His head begins to thump. He feels chilled right through. Dropping the notebook he goes to his rucksack and drags out a thick winter shirt, then gives the rucksack a great shove across the floor.

Alvie mumbles; opens her eyes. 'Up already?'

'It isn't exactly early.'

'What's eating you?'

'I've got a headache.'

'Bad? How bad?'

'It's like those snakes wound around old man Laocoön,' he tells her, rather pleased with that, glancing across at her as he buttons his cuffs.

She laughs. 'It's probably all that Chianti you've been drinking. You want to watch it, Phil.' She yawns, stretches, pushes her hair off her face. Pulling a blanket around herself she comes across to the window. 'Want me to rub your head?'

'Yes please.' Head against her breast he tells her, 'When I woke up in the middle of the night I couldn't remember where I was. It was horrible.' It is the ghost of a childhood terror: waking to a darkness that gave him back nothing but his screams until, alarmed, impatient, blinking as she switched on his light, his mother would rush in.

Alvie's fingertips on his temples move in slow firm circles. 'You soon remembered,' she says drily.

'You smell good,' he murmurs, breathing in a mixture of sleepiness and yesterday's sweat and the ardour of his pre-dawn clinging.

She laughs again. 'So do you. Maybe that's it – compatible whatsits-names.' His hands take in the familiar sharpness of her hip bones, the smoothness of skin. Her thighs part slightly. She says, 'Where are we off to today, Phil – the Accademia, is it? What's so funny?'

'You. Saying that. Where are we off to today. Remember that first holiday you spent at my father's when we were kids and I was supposed to be showing you the sights of Melbourne?' Like wine there courses through him memories of that frantic two weeks; those old things he loved that he wanted to show her, and the first time she touched him (it was outside the Museum), and the kisses and fondling that nearly sent him crazy until on the very last night of her visit she said yes to him (he cleaned his teeth first, he remembers), a scared kid discovering with her what other kids sniggered about and poets sang about and his parents wrecked up his childhood fighting about. And himself? She had whispered, 'Quick, get something, anything, yes, your singlet'll do' because she was bleeding. Loving her he had made her bleed. But she hadn't cared, she'd said, 'Don't be shocked, Philip. I'd rather it was you than anyone,' and he had cried with the joy of her.

'I remember.' The blanket slips from her shoulders as she waves her hand at their pile of guidebooks and mementoes. 'So here we are. So what's new?'

He looks at her, sees the delicacy of marble. An idea hits him. 'That statue of Apollo pursuing Daphne in that gallery in Rome – you know, the one by Bernini –' They had walked around it for ages, marvelling at the desperation the sculptor had caught, the cry for help, the youthful arms outstretched, the swirling cloak covering the lust doomed to marble imprisonment forever as the nymph's flesh turns to wood at his touch.

'The letch with the hots for the leafy lady – that one?'

It's the poet clutching at his muse, he thinks excitedly. Scooping up his notebook and scrawling 'Bern's Ap → Daph = me → inspiration', he tells her, 'I know exactly how frustrated that poor bugger felt!'

For a moment she stares at him, then pulling on her tracksuit and snatching up towel and soap she retorts, 'Oh you do, do you? Just what *do* you think happened when you woke me up at four o'clock this morning?'

But whether she is offended or pretending he's not sure because when he starts to explain what he meant she shuts him up with one of her kisses, and when he grabs her towel to pull her onto the bed with him she turns it into a wrestling match, which she wins by escaping into the passage.

(2) Odalisque

Breakfast in the pensione is served until nine.

It is now twenty past.

Philip, arranging his damp shirt on a hanger by the window, says, 'It's hardly worth going down, is it?' but Alvie, pulling a comb once through her wet hair, jangles the room key at him, saying, 'Come *on*, we're paying aren't we?'

On the stairs maids are bundling heaps of linen. 'Permesso!' she calls, bounding past them. 'Bon jerno! Kommy star? Permesso!' '*Bon giorno, bon giorno!*' he echoes, relishing her easy warmth with strangers but wincing at her accent. In the dining-room doorway they pause. The room is almost empty, the other guests well on their way to the Uffizi or the Ponte Vecchio by now. A waitress glances at them then goes on shaking cloths and laying clean cutlery.

She nudges him. 'Me dispee-archie,' she mews plaintively, then drops her head to her folded hands in a parody of sleeping. 'Troppo! Troppo!' She nudges him again triumphantly as the waitress, sighing, waves them to a table by the window. 'Wow! Just look at that sunshine, will you!' she exclaims, pulling the lace curtain aside so that he sees a brightening in the grey sky. 'We're dead lucky, aren't we?' She peers at him around a fold of the curtain, her eyes round. 'What if someone . . .' They burst out laughing. Under the table her feet find his.

He glances around the room. Is the waitress grinning? Is that disgust crossing the faces of the middle-aged couple whose eye he catches? He looks down at his hands, momentarily convinced that what he still feels in his fingertips, his joints, along all his senses, must be apparent to everyone – his hurrying with her towel to the shower cubicle at the end of the corridor and finding the door ajar because the lock doesn't catch and her saying, 'Oh it's *you*, is it?' goggling her eyes at him around the plastic curtain then catching his shirt sleeve and trying to pull him into the shower recess with her, laughing at his protests as his clean shirt gets soaked, and then the two of them together in the shower fighting over the miserable trickle of hot water, feet skidding on the mouldy floor, hip bones jostling, her body slippery with soap, tasting of soap, opening to his urgency as though it's five years not five hours since they last made love, water spraying everywhere and should someone barge in only the greasy plastic shower curtain dividing love from indecency.

The waitress brings two rolls and two pastries to their table. 'Go on,' Alvie says, biting into one of them. 'Eat up, they'll be giving us the shove in a minute.'

'Coffee? Tea?' the waitress asks.

'Kaffay con lattay,' she replies, indicating him. It's something they agreed on before they left home: to use their little bit of Italian wherever they could; they'd feel part of the place then; it would be more fun. '*Si, un caffè con latte*,' he repeats. '*Per favore*.' But while he struggles to find the correct word, the correct way to hold his mouth, she slams the phrase-book shut and plunges on. She points to herself. 'Daisy dayro ... daisy dayro tay con lattay freddo. *Freddo!*' she emphasises. 'I can't stomach tea with hot milk,' she tells him, and she pulls another of her faces, looking to him to laugh with her – but at what? at funny foreign customs? at herself for being so pigheaded over cold milk in the cup first? He isn't sure. But laughs anyway, because looking at her he is reminded of a plant his stepmother grows in a sunny garden bed, a joyous plant all pinks and reds and golds among the dark green leaves of its neighbours. It catches him with a shock of gladness each time he passes it. Love-lies-bleeding, his stepmother calls it. Philip prefers amaranthus, a name he looked up in the dictionary once because he liked the sound of it: *amaranth, an imaginary unfading flower*. Watching Alvie now as she drowns a spoonful of brown sugar then chews it, the sort of silly thing you remember years later about people, he thinks excitedly love is like that plant, not imaginary meaning unreal but *imagined, of the imagination* – five minutes fucking somewhere, bed-room, bathroom, each moment gone as it's happening, but the joy of it lasting, shaped in your mind the way all the canvas and stone we've been looking at these last few days has been worked on, shaped: a glimpse of the unimaginable.

'Maybe we should catch a bus,' she is saying, leaning over the table to look at his watch. Her own watch is probably on the floor somewhere upstairs, one of her careless, carefree habits. 'If we don't sit down for a cappuccino, maybe we can afford a bus?'

'Yes,' he says, concentrating on the spoon he is turning in his cup. He wants her again. When they go upstairs to clean their teeth, he will have her again. And there rises the certainty that from all the notes, bits of verse, impressions filling page after page of his notebook he will shape a poem more erotic than anything he has yet tried, a poem as voluptuous as worked marble, as sensual as Titian's Venus yesterday, the glowing flesh turned in love to whoever looked at her, as unfading as an imaginary flower.

(3) Madonna

'It'll be good,' he tells her as they climb onto the crowded bus. 'It'll be different.' Alvie pulls him towards two seats about to be vacated. 'It'll combine everything I've felt about all this – this –' And he gestures widely to indicate: *everything*. Words spin into his mind. He begins to juggle phrases. So absorbed is he, staring into the aisle at nothing, that it is Alvie who sees them first. 'Look!' she says, nudging him. 'That cap on that girl – isn't it great?'

He looks. Along the narrow medieval footpath, walking in the same direction as the slow-moving bus, come two girls wearing jeans and leather jackets, sisters perhaps, one about twelve who is talking, gesticulating, skipping around people in her way, the other older, taller, her fair hair falling to her shoulders from under her Mao cap, and her hands as calm as her still, grave face. Where have they come from? Perhaps they live in one of these ancient jutting houses. If it were not for their clothes, he thinks, looking from one to the other as they catch up with the bus, they might have stepped out of a fifteenth-century painting. The bus crawls past, then stops altogether. Horns toot. Ahead he can see a policeman waving his arms. He looks back at the girls, and sees a youth carrying a satchel and a rolled-up tube of paper approach the older girl and speak. She stops. *The Angel Gabriel at the Annunciation*, he thinks. The Angel Gabriel unrolls his scroll of paper and displays it. He has long dark hair and a soft cap like an upturned plant pot – 'Like the cap we saw in that painting yesterday!' Philip exclaims. 'That Lippi self-portrait, remember?' Painted by the artist-son of an artist-priest and the nun Lucretia . . . 'Fra Filippo Lippi used to hop out of his monastery at night and rage around Florence – along this street maybe, Alvie!' He cranes across her.

She breathes into his neck, 'Some guy, that Filippo. Looking for inspiration, was he? I got a postcard of his Madonna, Phil,' she adds, sitting up. 'You know, the one with the little angel peeking over his shoulder?'

'Did you? It's lovely, isn't it?' Lucretia was probably the model for that painting. Philip likes to think so anyway. He sees the priest at his easel, splotches of paint on his black garb, capturing forever the girl he has smuggled into his cell. Look at the Christ-Child, he tells them. You must all look at the Christ-Child. Lucretia, dazed with his kisses, folds her quivering hands and lowers her eyes, but one of the little Angels won't keep his head still . . .

It's Fra Filippo out there and he wants to paint her. The youth and the girl confer earnestly. As the youth takes more papers from his satchel, the younger girl, the little sister, looks from one to the other with, well not a smirk exactly, smirk's a bit coarse –

At last the girl gives back the sheets of paper, reluctantly Philip thinks, and the youth rolls them up again. Fastening his satchel he goes on his way. Just then the bus lurches forward through a gap in the traffic, and Philip's last sight of them is of the little sister laughing outright, and the girl glancing over her shoulder at God's messenger, curious and secretly pleased –

'Dirty postcards, I bet,' says his Madonna, shoving him in the ribs with her elbow.

(4) The Slaves

Hunching their shoulders, they cross the piazza. It is weather for moving briskly, but two middle-aged women in black have stopped to chat under the bare trees, their hands in fingerless gloves, bread and vegetables clutched in their arms. Their laughter rings like metal. A few people, off-season tourists like Alvie and Philip perhaps, are gazing up at the facade of the great church, or poring over maps. Pigeons fly down to a child who is scattering a few crumbs. At the rapid approach of a black-robed priest, his heavy cross swinging, the pigeons fly up in a swoop of wings, then settle again hungrily. One white pigeon, however, does not fly down with the others but flaps and whirrs between the trees in a dazzle of white wings. As it turns gracefully above their heads Alvie cries, 'Oh look, Phil!' then laughs out loud as it comes to land in front of the child, a plastic wind-up toy. 'I thought it was *real!*' And she links her arm in his and squeezes, a gesture that says, Aren't I silly, and isn't that bird silly, and isn't all this *fun?*

As they get closer to the child scattering crumbs, Philip notices a very tall, very thin black man approaching. With one long arm the man scoops up the bird then stands quite still, not speaking to the child who has begun to stalk a real pigeon – not speaking to Alvie or Philip either, hardly looking at them, but by the way he is standing as aware of them as they are of him. His thin black fingers caress the plastic toy. It is one of those moments, Philip thinks, one of those moments that means more than itself, the women's conversation that I can almost understand and the child hunting and the black man with the white bird, waiting. I'll buy it for Alvie as a memento, for fun.

As he hesitates, adding up lire in his head, he hears an Australian voice saying, 'Jesus, this world!' Turning, he finds a young man with a rucksack standing just behind him. 'He does that every day,' says the stranger, giving a nod towards the black man. 'Him and dozens of others like him all over Europe. Haven't you seen them? They're slaves — yes, slaves,' he repeats at Alvie's startled look. 'There's a boss man somewhere around; he brings these people into the country and provides the bits of plastic and a shed for them to doss down in, and out they go, every day, tourists or no tourists, trying to earn a few cents because they're all wanting to get back home, especially now that winter's coming on and winter in Europe's not much fun if you come from a warm place, but they haven't got a hope, they'll never earn their fare back again, the best they can hope for is enough to eat and a place to sleep and if they don't manage to sell any the boss man kicks them out and they starve.'

On hearing this Philip thinks, I couldn't bear that bird now, I'll just *give* him the money. But as he struggles in his mind for the right words in Italian, I want . . . I do not want, the black man abruptly launches the plastic toy into the air and follows it to the other side of the piazza, and the opportunity is lost.

'We're off to see David,' Alvie is saying to the stranger. 'The Accademia's just around the corner.'

The stranger nods. 'Me too. I'll tag along with you.' He shrugs his shoulders to ease the rucksack decorated with a blue and white Eureka flag, that symbol of freedom. He looks as though he's been travelling a long time. His boots are worn down to the uppers, his jeans in tatters, Philip observes, glancing down at his own neat jeans bought for this trip. His untrimmed beard and his hair tangling onto his shoulders make Philip think of a satyr, one of those hairy half-creatures of the woods and fields that he and Alvie have been looking at in dozens of paintings and sculptures over the last few days. Marsyas, he thinks. The satyr Marsyas – the one that painters loved because he challenged the god Apollo and got skinned alive. He hears Marsyas tell Alvie, 'David was carved out of the one big block of stone. They say that when Michelangelo looked at it he could see David there in it, waiting to get out.'

'Is that so?' exclaims Alvie, opening her eyes wide – and Philip raises his eyebrows to himself, since it was only yesterday that Alvie herself read that bit of information out loud from a guide book in a bookshop.

Philip stands for a long time in front of Michelangelo's first Slave, one of four in this gallery, marvelling at the anguished effort in the powerful shoulders and stomach muscles as the imprisoned man struggles against his bondage of stone. Michelangelo never finished it, Philip thinks, but it looks just right the way it is – the figure trapped, straining, not whole yet, desperate to stand free like the David.

He looks around to tell Alvie . . . and sees that she has already finished looking at the four Slaves, and not only the Slaves but the highlight of the gallery, David standing in the floodlit niche. She is slouching with her back to the Pietà of Michelangelo's old age, the one Philip read makes an interesting comparison with the highly polished one in the Vatican. She is talking to the stranger.

Moving closer he hears her saying in the bantering tone that annoys her when other women use it to men, 'Okay, so Jesus' legs are deliberately sculpted all rough, not even the same length, so you tell me why.'

'Because Michelangelo was in a hurry, he was afraid he might die before he finished,' Philip puts in quickly.

The stranger glances at him. 'When people were crucified, hanging there was such agony they used to push up with their feet against the nail to get a few seconds' relief, so the soldiers would come around with clubs and break their legs so that they couldn't.'

'God!' Alvie exclaims. 'Why are people so vile to one another? Did you know that?'

Philip shakes his head. 'Have you had a good look at the David?' he asks as she makes to move towards the door.

The stranger, turning with her, says over his shoulder, 'Take a look at David from the side. There's real apprehension on his face. You don't get that on the postcards.'

Philip catches Alvie's eye. 'Come and look?

'No. You.' She glances back at the half-formed torsos and the beaten corpse. 'I'm going outside for a bit.'

He shrugs, and takes longer than he means to over the rest of the sculpture. When he comes out of the gallery he finds her sitting alone on the steps.

'Let's go.'

'Hang on,' she says. 'I'm minding his rucksack.'

He notices it then, the grimy worn rucksack with the Eureka flag. 'Is *he* still hanging around?'

'What's eating you?'

He says nothing to that, just sits beside her on the cold step and watches the black man throwing the plastic pigeon.

(5) Triptych

'This one,' Alvie says, peering in through the window of the locanda. 'All the people in here look like locals.' An elderly waiter escorts them to a table and pulls out their chairs with a flourish. Alvie, laughing up at the man, insists on giving the three orders in her atrocious Italian. Three, because the stranger is still tagging along. Marsyas. The satyr with the Eureka flag. When Philip said to Alvie on the gallery steps, 'So let's get something to drink. Okay?' *he* said as he hoisted up his rucksack, 'Good idea. What about something a bit more substantial?'

Philip mentally calculates lire again. One good meal a day. And a bottle of wine. He sees Eureka Flag top up his glass – tops up his own.

Eureka Flag is telling Alvie that he's on his way home. Back to an Australian summer. He's been wandering around Europe for months.

'I suppose you've been in every gallery and cathedral,' Philip says enviously. It's the first thing he has said to him.

The guy says no he hasn't, as a matter of fact this is the first gallery he's bothered with, but he thought he'd better see something to tell his family. He doesn't go for this sort of thing as a rule, there are too many terrible things going on in the world to be wasting his time in old tombs and churches, we might all be blown up tomorrow the way things are heading.

'All the more reason,' Philip replies, warming to the debate, 'for seeing all this before it disappears. It doesn't seem logical not to,' he continues eagerly. 'I mean, here are all these marvellous things around you that have inspired people for centuries – ordinary people, I mean, as well as all sorts of artists – and either way you're going to miss out, aren't you? Either by being blown up, which might not happen anyway, or by worrying yourself silly beforehand –' And he gives him a rundown on all the things he's missing right here in Florence, the Loggia for instance, an open-air museum full of statues of old Greek legends, Hercules breaking a Centaur's neck, and the Rape of someone, two rapes actually, and Perseus with the head of Medusa. And the Baptistry doors – he mustn't miss the Baptistry doors, especially Ghiberti's, Paradise and murder and wrath and punishment in ten bronze panels.

Eureka Flag leans forward. 'Centuries of it, right? See, I've got this theory –'

'And the Cathedral,' Philip interrupts, splashing wine into their glasses. (Alvie puts her hand across hers.) 'The Cathedral – there's another Pietà there, a polished one like the one in the Vatican.' He racks his brain for something to cap the other's comment about the Pietà they saw this morning.

'What have you been doing?' Alvie asks.

He replies that he's just been to Germany for the autumn peace demonstrations. He was with the people blockading one of the American missile bases. When they started the blockade no one knew whether the police would play it low key or get heavy. Boy, water cannons are no joke!

'It doesn't seem like you've been having much of a fun time overseas,' Alvie comments, wrinkling up her nose. And she smiles at him. Chin propped on one hand. Smiling.

'Or achieving anything much,' Philip adds, turning to order more wine.

'Wrong!' says the guy. 'People like you two should go along to a demonstration sometime. See for yourselves. At the missile base,

for instance. Boy, was that something! All those blockaders working together, *caring* for each other. It's the only way, getting
together, showing other people. It's true what old JC said (not that
I'm religious or anything like that), Wherever two or three are
gathered together – like the three of us, say. That's all it takes
because before long two or three more will join in and soon you'll
have a crowd, you'll have a whole city, a nation – all because of two
or three. Only they've got to care, that first bunch, they've got to
get rid of all the fear inside themselves, all the anger, they've got
to love one another –' He smiles apologetically. 'Have you noticed
how easy it is to say you hate something, I hate the unions, but if
you start on about love everyone thinks you're some sort of
nutter?'

Alvie says, 'I love Ronald Reagan,' and laughs.

Philip tries to catch her eye: *We love each other.*

At that moment their meal arrives.

'That was quick,' Eureka Flag comments. He grins at Alvie. 'It
helps all right if you know the language.'

Alvie gives a little shrug of pleasure, a quick tightening of the
shoulders like a hug. 'And if you're a woman,' Philip smirks.

'Oh rubbish!' Alvie says. 'They just like you to try.'

Philip lifts his glass and studies the dark red wine. 'Especially if
you're a woman,' he repeats, watching sideways as the colour runs
into her face. He says softly, 'It wouldn't matter how badly you said
it.'

'*Get stuffed!*' Alvie breathes.

Eureka Flag is saying, 'Great nosh-up, this. If I hadn't found you
guys I'd have just grabbed a pizza somewhere.' He says are they
going to Germany, he can give them the name of friends to stay
with in Germany, they're great people, they live in a huge old con-
verted barn, so there's heaps of room, they'll make Alvie and Philip
welcome in Germany.

'Sounds great!' Alvie says. 'Phil?'

'Are we going to Germany?' Philip responds in what comes back
to him as the thin sarcastic tone he hasn't heard in years, his father's
to his mother, before they split up. So he says hastily, 'Yes, the
Loggia – he must see the Loggia, mustn't he, Alvie? – and just a few
steps away there's David again.' 'A replica,' Alvie explains. 'The
small force against the evil in the world!' Philip declaims,
flourishing his glass. He adds, 'With bird shit on his head!' And
laughs.

For a moment Alvie stares at him like a mother or something, then turns back to her plate. 'How's yours?' she asks the other guy. 'Want to try some of mine?' They exchange spoonfuls. Philip shrieks with silent laughter when a gob of pasta catches in his beard.

'Philip?'

'No thanks. I'm happy with what I've got.'

'Well – can I have a taste, then?' Alvie persists. Philip shrugs, and pushes his plate across the table. She asks, concentrating on her fork, 'Do you have brothers and sisters back home?' The guy's face lights up. Two sisters and a brother, he tells her. 'Uhuh,' says Alvie, nodding. She says, 'My Aunt Trudi's a teacher – you know? And she reckons you can always tell the kids without any brothers and sisters the day they come to school. They never want to lend their coloured pencils.'

'Is that so?' says Philip.

(6) Commedia dell'Arte

Philip, emptying the bottle into his glass, hears himself saying so heartily that Alvie starts staring again, 'So what are we all doing the rest of this afternoon? You could go to the Uffizi, mate, but it'll be closing time soon, and if you want to stick with us why don't we just walk around in the centre of town?' and Spaghetti Beard says, 'Great, mate!' so they're landed with him for the rest of the day. Philip, hogging the guidebook, shouts, 'The Loggia! Let's start with the Loggia!' but Marsyas the rebel jumps to his feet shouting, 'No, Paradise – that's where it all started, mate, all the aggro!'

'Alvie?' says Philip.

Alvie sits scraping up the dregs of her cappuccino with her spoon. Suddenly she bursts out, 'So where's it all getting us? That's what I'd like to know. All this cruelty, snakes crushing people, men racing off women or fighting half-horse things, Judith cutting off some guy's head I don't know how many times, some poor young guy shot full of arrows and looking *pleased* about it for Chrissake! – It's horrible, horrible, I don't care if I never see another bleeding Jesus!'

They are silent for some minutes then. She goes on scraping the bottom of her cup until Philip has to stop himself reaching over and taking it from her because when he was a child his mother would never let him do that.

'Let's go back to the big square,' suggests their companion. 'There's usually something happening in the squares, even at this time of year.' Street theatre, he tells them – he was into a bit of street theatre himself with the peace movement. Sure enough, in the piazza people are gathering around a young woman who has lighted some sort of flare in a tin and is blowing bubbles. Flickering light catches at the bubbles as they float off into the dusk. Two or three children run with upstretched arms. Suddenly the woman puts down the bubble pipe and reaching out catches one, two, three, four bubbles and begins to juggle them, her eyes dark pits in her uplifted face. A murmur runs through the crowd. Somebody claps. At the sound her hands falter. One of the bubbles drops and bounces once, twice, on the pavement.

Leaning forward without looking down the woman catches the bubble and tosses it back with the others – gobs of colour pulled together into a pattern of light.

'Oh!' Alvie cries, delighted. 'Now how does she do that?'

It's just what I'm trying to do with words! Philip thinks, or does he shout it, because Alvie and Spaghetti Beard begin to laugh; all around people are laughing, staring at him, and he burns with embarrassment, hearing himself sound pretentious, ridiculous. He hates her for joining in with that fellow in mocking him. He turns away quickly – and sees what they have all been guffawing at. It is not him at all, but a young man behind him, right at his shoulder, another of these street theatre characters, a mimic this time. Philip, turning, catches him leaning forward earnestly, just as Philip must have been leaning, a frightful frown on his face. As he turns the young man jumps away and begins to mince across the piazza behind a woman wearing extraordinarily high heels. Each time the woman half-glances over one shoulder, conscious of something out of place, the mimic steps to the other shoulder, so artful you can see those high heels on his mocking ankles. This time Philip joins in the laughter, even throwing a few hundred lire when the man brings around his cap, but the noise screams in his ears.

(7) Love Lies Bleeding or The Muse Nailed

'Let's go!' he says as Marsyas moves off to look at the huge white

Neptune dominating the piazza. Not yet, Alvie replies. He can if he wants, but there's plenty happening here, she's going to hang about for a bit.

'With him?'

'He's okay. He's nice. You stay too.'

'What for? I can't see anything happening. Come on. I don't want to hang around any more.'

She shrugs his hand off her arm. 'Well maybe I do.'

Marsyas comes back to them. 'You two coming?'

He hovers indecisively. 'I want to do a bit of writing,' he says, looking at Alvie.

'Letters home,' says Marsyas.

He would let it go at that but Alvie says, 'No, poems, he writes poems, he's working on something right now, but he won't let anyone see till it's finished. He's good,' she adds. 'He gets things published.'

'Only in things no one's ever heard of,' he says modestly.

'What do you write about?'

'Love poems,' Alvie replies as he hesitates, so that he feels himself going red again.

'You should write about real things,' says Marsyas. 'I mean, like what's going on around us in this stuffed up world. The sort of things those guys –' He gestures towards the marble figures in the Loggia – 'have been rabbiting on about for centuries. Only now it's pollution and Pershing missiles. Same thing, isn't it? You're good, she says – you might change something.'

'I'll keep it in mind,' Philip replies, furious with her, with both of them.

Back in the room at the pensione he sits on the bed under the bare globe and on a fresh page of his notebook writes 'Art mocks Life'. Or should it be the other way around? 'Life stuffs up Art'. Then he sits for a long time tapping the pencil. How can she just wander off till all hours in a foreign city with some yobbo she knows nothing about? *Satyr holds orgy in bed-and-breakfast. Sabine woman seized, rescuer trampled.* He writes 'Life' again then sits turning the pencil point in the dot over the *i*. The minute she sets foot in this room he will grab her, rip off leaves and bark to the heartwood, screw her till she screams, screw that satyr out of her, flay him alive in front of her, shoot her full of arrows, thorns, nails, break her legs –

He begins to write. The pencil races. When he has finished there appears a poem that leaves him drained and triumphant but is so ugly, so violent, that as he rereads it he feels sick. Throwing pencil and notebook onto the floor he crawls into bed. He is awakened later – minutes? hours?– by muffled laughter, the turning of the door handle, more squawks of laughter. 'Put the light on,' he says coldly. 'I'm not asleep.' The glare almost blinds him but he can make her out, alive with laughter, and behind her, standing in the doorway clutching his rucksack, *him.*

'He's got nowhere to sleep,' she says. 'He had to vacate his room yesterday morning, so I said he could camp here overnight.'

'Oh sure,' he replies. 'Help yourself. Room in this bed for three. Edge or middle?'

But sarcasm is wasted on *him.* 'No worries, the floor's fine by me,' says the satyr, and begins to unroll a thin grubby mat and a sleeping bag.

She titters again. 'You should have heard me chatting up the guy on the desk so he wouldn't notice him sneaking upstairs!'

When he wakes again, head aching, groin aching, it is almost daylight. The intruder has gone. Mat, sleeping bag, rucksack – gone. He turns his head; Alvie is still asleep. As he slides his hand between her thighs she murmurs half-waking and puts her arms around him. When they have made love they turn back to back, their bottoms touching. From the edge of the bed he sees his notebook lying open on the floor, and remembers with amazement his poem of last night – too shameful to show anyone, too good to tear up. As light seeps into the room he can make out several pencilled arrows pointing to something scrawled under his own writing. Leaning out to reach it, he reads, 'Thanx!' and an address in Germany.

Telephone Conversation in a Common Language

Sandra Shotlander

Uh ha, um, yes, oh. . . just a minute. Is that the Cathy of Cathy and Trish or Cathy and Joy? The other Cathy, not Cathy and Trish or Cathy and Joy – oh, Cathy and Jane, the Jane who used to live with Barb, Barb of Susie and Barb. Susie was Jenny's ex-lover. Yes, I know Jenny of Jenny, Terry and Pat, yes, and Pat and Fay and Fay and Cathy.

Yes, the same Cathy, no, not the Cathy of Cathy and Trish or Cathy and Joy, the Cathy of Cathy and Jane who used to live with Barb of Susie and Barb. Susie was Jenny's lover, the Jenny of Jenny, Terry and Pat before Pat was with Fay and Fay and Cathy and Fay and Jane and Fay and Barb.

What do you mean? They weren't? Fay wasn't ever Barb's lover they were just co-counsellors? Yes, I know Barb changed her name to Rose Ella, when she went to the hills, and Cathy of Cathy and Trish is Autumn River, and Trish is Lightning Ridge now, didn't you know? And then Jenny and Terry and Pat are Calliope, Terpsichore and Urania after the three muses, and Cathy and Joy have gone Celtic, and Fay's Morgan le Fay since she became a witch, and Susie can't make up her mind. Did you know, she's thinking of changing. She's calling herself Susie Cambio, which means Susie Changing in Italian.

Autumn River, Lightning Ridge and Terpsichore. It worries me, you know. Well, of course I believe in women choosing their own names, but it ruins the flow of a good telephone conversation.

Anyway, what did the naturopath say? You didn't go. You went to what? An orthomolecular specialist. What's that? Oh, allergies. And what have you got? Dust, grasses, yes, pollens, flowers, cat's fur, that's bad, tomatoes, avocadoes, strawberries, stone fruit, dairy, wheat, flour, detergents, Germicidal Dot, boot polish and burnt toast. There's not much left really, is there? I mean, it's hardly worth living. And the tests can be negative, but you're still allergic. Why do you have the tests then? I see. So you can have them again if they turn up negative.

You sound very elsewhere. Aren't I? I'm not the only one who's commented. Who've you been talking to? Is that the Cathy of Cathy and Trish or Cathy and . . . it doesn't matter. You know that's the third time you've mentioned Cathy. There isn't anything? I mean, I know it's absolutely none of my business, since we became ex-lovers, since we have transcended our sexual ties and taken our space. I just thought we were both into celibacy, radical celibates.

I know, I do understand, you've told me six hundred times, it's good for me to be on my own and I do meditate a lot on my trolloping around in my past lives. It's just that I'm alive now, and you're on the other end of this thin wire connecting us and you seem to be in another world.

You know, Fay, that is, Morgan le Fay, rang me the other day. Asked me if I'd ever had a sexual experience where you went out of your body. Have you? No, I haven't either. She has, but then she's not in this world very much at any time.

You do sound very elsewhere. What are you doing? I can hear purring. You're giving the cat reiki massage on her broken tail. I see, the energy you put out comes right back. Well, that's certainly an improvement on having relationships. No, really, I'd like to try it, I would, on my broken parts, but, you see, I'm really hoping to get to that place in meditation where I don't need touch. I could become a social revolutionary and give up emotion altogether.

Who told you that? No I didn't. I did not. I didn't cry on anyone's shoulder. I wish you wouldn't say things like that. You know all the Cancer in my chart makes me vulnerable.

She told you, did she? She would. She's beyond help. She's not, she's straight. She'd wash a man's feet and dry them with that long hair of hers. Just grovels. I'll bet she's in a self-devised drama. Her life's one big self-devised drama, if you ask me. Look, I know you think the only drama in the world is self-devised, whatever that means. Anyway, what's this got to do with healing? Did you notice the full moon last night? You were pre-menstrual. Pop over for a bit of brown rice and lentils or a hunk of chocolate cake, if you like, and you can show me the reiki massage. Funny, you'll have to get rid of the cat now that they've told you you're allergic to it. And, speaking about separating, did you hear about Margaret and Teena? Well, are they or aren't they? I mean, they were together at Susie's party and apart at the women's ball. Yes, what about Fiona and Paula and Rainbow and . . .

A Fantasy

Jesse Kate Blackadder

her head, round and small, and that soft sweet smell of baby   perfect skin, round and smooth and smelling so new no old smells have had a chance   just that round head fitting my hand   my nipple touching her cheek and her head turns   blind instinct   eyes closed   mouth gasping open, finding the nipple   the warm smell of milk suckling   the milk coming to my breast   coming up feel it all the way down   breast aching to her mouth heart swelling   uterus contracting pleasure   deeply her hand on soft skin   mouth fitting to nipple   aching I need you   tiny hand curling   eyes closed   sucking fiercely everything flowing   surrendering   blood moving   holding   head fits into my hand   breasts swell   the first time, the first child to suck, and the hand is still, her head fits in my palm, her lips slow, sucking slows, sleeping, mouth loosening, traces of milk around pink full lips

THE INVISIBLE HAND

Stephanie Johnson

The lights are on time release. I can flick the switch with my left hand while maintaining a hold on slippery Macha, and keeping the fingers of my right hand curled round the handle of the pushchair. Then we have precisely three minutes to get up the three flights of stairs, open the door – and there's always a struggle to find the keys – and get inside. Sometimes I have to leave bags of groceries at the bottom and must wait the two-minute time lag before I can flick the switch again, before the lights will come on, before I can get groceries, and return to my Macha who by this time is removing every item of clothing from her round body including possibly soiled nappies, adding to the chaos. Chaos is a word my mother would use if she could see where we live, but she can't because she lives in New Zealand.

Macha and I don't go out much, except to the bank and the shops two or three times a week, and the park on the way to the post office. At the post office I clear my mailbox. I run a kind of a business. Social Security doesn't know about my business, which is just as well.

The business wasn't my idea. Sometimes these things just appear like gifts, or babies.

One night, before Macha could walk, I was lying down in the other room. It was winter and I felt just as dark and heavy as the rain outside. In preparation for times like this I had written helpful sentences on the wall around the bed.

I am Robyn – A Strong Woman
I am Robyn – Life-Giver and Mother

I am Robyn – Artist
I am Robyn – An Independent and Free-Spirited Woman

Tonight the phrases glance off my eyeballs. They don't even permeate to my brain, let alone my heart. Macha is crying and I hate her. She's been crying all day, one of her cheeks the bright red heralder of a new tooth. My sympathy for her has ebbed. Then, suddenly, the phone rings.

I don't mind admitting I have few friends. My mother never phones. Sometimes Reece calls. Reece is the father of my son, and the judge gave him custody. Macha's father never phones. I only knew him for one night.

Macha stares at me, her mouth open but silent. Could it be that she already understands that telephones must be answered?

In the kitchen the floor is awash from the pissing washing-machine. My thongs suck their way across to the bench.

'Hello.'

There is nobody there. But just as I think about replacing the hand-set I discern a breathing. A breathing getting hoarser.

'Who is it?'

The breathing is interspersed with groans. There is a man coming, somewhere in the city, into my telephone.

I hang up loudly, in his ear. Macha uses the click as a cue to resume her yowling.

The next night is an action replay, although Macha's cheek is not so red and a tiny tip of tooth is presenting itself, and the man on the phone takes longer to come. I am surprised at myself for tolerating it. Perhaps I feel sorry for him. Men are so primitive, with it all hanging out of their bodies. At least I will not conceive from his attentions, through the ear, like an Elizabethan cat. And it is a good way to check that the phone still works.

My admirer calls most nights.

Then there is a day which is eventful. Macha takes her first steps and sleeps that night exhausted. I am shunting the furniture around for something to do, when the phone rings.

'Hello.'

There is complete silence, not even the breathing.

'Are you there?'

Of course, it needn't necessarily be the same bloke, I reason.

'You'll have to help me tonight.'

I am stunned – like a radio play with a lot of pauses I have finally heard his voice. He is American. Perhaps he is old.

'Can you hear me?' he asks.

'Yes.'

'The mind is willing, but the flesh is weak – do you get me?'

'Of course.' Although neither Reece nor Macha's father ever demonstrated this condition to me.

'Will you help me?'

'How?'

'Talk,' he says. 'Tell me what you look like.'

'Well, I'm . . .'

'Faster.'

'I'm tall, and I'm – I suppose I'm big, and –'

'What colour are your eyes?'

'Green.'

'Hair?'

'Brown.'

'How old are you?'

'Twenty-six.'

He comes. I put down the phone. I make a decision. The next time the phone rings late at night, I won't answer it.

Macha has to go to the doctor in half an hour. She keeps throwing up. I am hunting for the Medicare card, and loathing my predicament. I wonder if the receptionist will believe I have one if I tell her about it. The phone rings.

'Hello.'

'You don't know me, but I've been calling you in the evenings.'

I am suddenly finely sprayed with water, from the inside, and my heart is thumping.

'I have a proposal to make. Are you interested?'

Macha covers the front of her jumper with green bile.

'I can't talk now. My kid is being sick.'

'You have a child?' He sounds disappointed.

'Two.' That ought to put him off.

'You are in need of a little financial assistance then?'

What's he after? I'm frightened. Perhaps he knows where I live. I hang up.

But he doesn't let me get out the door. As soon as Macha is in a clean top he calls again. For the first time in . . . I can't remember how long, I'm angry.

'Leave me alone.'

'I'll give you five thousand dollars to start a club. There are other men who would use you.'

'What do you mean?' Five thousand dollars?

He laughs. He is American, he is a man, and he is obviously rich. He knows the power of money.

'A wanker's club.' I think he has what they call a Southern drawl. 'I belonged to one in the States.'

'What is it?' I ask. I pick Macha up.

'You get yourself a post office box. I'll send you the money. You'll have to advertise. Men will send you money and book a call. You'll learn business sense. Never accept a call without the money in your pocket.'

Macha is grizzling again. I am appalled at the degree of my temptation.

'Where do I advertise?'

'In any of the men's magazines.' He thinks I'm very stupid.

'Why are you doing this?' I ask. 'What do you get out of it?'

'I'll call again.' For the first time he hangs up first.

I begin to dream. I dream of a car, nothing special, just a car. I dream of a little house for Macha and me. I picture an air ticket home to see my mother.

After we see the doctor I go to the post office to get myself a box. I tell the girl it's for 'The Invisible Hand Ltd', and I laugh. I spend a few dollars on a copy of *Ribald*.

Then, surprisingly, the American is true to his word. I open a bank account under my business name, and deposit the money. Macha and I have new clothes and I drive an old Volkswagen. I invest the rest.

One morning he rings me to tell me the ad is in *Ribald*. He is pleased with me but disappointed that I haven't used my real name.

'You have more business sense than I thought,' he says. 'Where do you live?'

'It doesn't matter where I live.' Talking to this man is getting easier.

'Don't you think we should meet?' He hasn't sounded like this before – pleading, boyish.

'No.' I am firm.

In the first week I receive nine bookings, and they all ring. Some of them want to talk, but most of them are only interested in a swift ejaculation. I charge ten dollars a time. Business picks up to the rate of seven or eight calls a night, and Macha learns to sleep through the ringing.

At the end of summer I put a deposit down on a little house. To celebrate I invite two of the mothers from the park round for an afternoon cup of coffee. The kitchen is sunny, and I have made an effort to clean it up.

At four o'clock the phone rings. An early booking – it had completely slipped my mind.

'Aren't you going to answer it?' asks Sue, whose nose had wrinkled noticeably when she entered my home.

'No, I'll let it ring,' I say, stirring sugar into my coffee. 'I know who it is.'

'Who?' asks Frances, seated gingerly on a pile of newspapers. The copy of *Ribald* lies near her right foot. She hasn't noticed it.

'A business acquaintance,' I say. 'More coffee anyone?'

He hangs up. Sue and Frances look at each other meaningfully. Perhaps they think I'm whoring. Sue lights a cigarette, and I find her a saucer for the ash. She begins to tell us about her holiday up the Gold Coast with her man, when the phone starts again.

'Will you answer it this time?' asks Frances.

I do. I go though the whole act in front of them. This chap is a regular, and he needs a lot of coaxing. I coax him. Sue has flushed scarlet and is staring at me.

Then he is finished, and I put down the phone. Sue and Frances are statues of their former selves. The children babble in the bedroom.

'Oliver,' calls Sue. She is shoving her cigarettes into her bag. I notice she has woman-signs dangling from her ears. She goes into the bedroom, and through the open door I can see her reading my sentences on the wall.

Frances clears her throat.

'How can you do that?' she asks. 'Doesn't it make you feel sick?'

'Not really.' It had never occurred to me to feel sick.

Sue has Oliver by the hand. He has felt-tip all over his face, and it looks suspiciously like Macha's handiwork. She is glowering at me.

'I . . . um . . . I was a social worker before I had Oliver,' she says, all of the we-are-oppressed-women-together gone out of her voice completely, 'and I wonder if it isn't a good idea for me to take Macha with me now.'

'What? Why?' All the blood in my body is in my feet. If I'd known she was an ex-social worker I would never have invited her.

'You're unfit to be a –' she begins.

I am looking at her Gold Coast suntan. I am looking at this hole in the wall that I've made into a home for Macha and me ever since Macha was born. I am thinking about Reece and Macha's father who was stronger than I was even though he was drunk. I am thinking about all these poor silly bastards who can't wank without a bit of help. I am so furious I have to laugh. Sue's biggest worry is balancing her heterosexuality with her politics. I know this because she told me.

'You're mad,' she's saying now. 'What are you laughing at? What you're doing is terrible – you have no need to do it – you're on the benefit aren't you?' There's a crack in her voice.

'Shut up,' Frances says to Sue. Slowly she gets up and comes across to me, smiling. She shakes my hand, collects her child, and pushes Sue and Oliver out ahead of her. At the door she turns.

'Is that how you got the house?' she asks.

I nod.

'Good on you,' she says.

I raise my coffee cup in a salute.

'I'm giving it up soon,' I say. But she's gone.

Macha and I are happy enough in our little house. We have a garden and a dog. There are no more phone calls but once a week I go into Grace Brothers and buy a dozen pairs of panties. The saleswomen are beginning to recognise me. Perhaps they think I have a panty fetish. I sell each pair for thirty dollars, after an hour's wear.

I wouldn't recommend my line of business for everyone. In a funny sort of way it's like the time-release lights in the stairwell in our old place. Nothing lasts for ever.

On the wall in my new bedroom it says,

I am a Strong, Free-Spirited Woman.
I Control My Own Destiny.

FUGUE ON FORTY

Sara Dowse

1   The man I am leaving has pale hair but interesting eyes. The kind that turn green with yellows, browns or greens, and stay fixed a dazzling blue with blue, like the sea on a bright spring day. They seem small, close together when he's tired, as though he hasn't the strength to hold them in place. Away from me, they are wide-spaced and large. Happy, innocent eyes. (I have seen them at parties.)

We fight, unhealthily. Crazy maelstroms that suck us in and blow us about and leave the waters clotted with hatred and suspicion.

I rarely sleep.

2   The man of my dreams has a pleasant, handsome face. Smooth in the centre, hard at the edge. Warm brown eyes – no ambivalence there. Ruddy beige of face. Curly black hair. A welcoming smile.

He says he remembers me.

I wonder.

1   Astigmatic, he sometimes shields his eyes with glasses. Heavy black rims on his wide, long face. They accentuate a rabbit look in him. He suffers from hay fever, wriggles his nose to keep them in place. When he wears them he looks cold, professional. Yet one is conscious of a disguise.

2   He says he will ring me. I admire his clothes. Caramel-coloured, to go with his face. He is an artist as I am. A musician. Baroque. We have friends in common. He will be coming to Canberra and will look me up. Pink and plump. A picture of health.

He might fit well in Canberra.

1   Our connections are crossed with brambles. His naked eye is a thistle. When we fight it's often because I wish it to end, or for there to be a sudden awakening, a realisation of love, a discovery, like the bright infant, floating pure and innocent through the bulrushes.

We fornicate, through this. Often quickly, but if he is angry, long and hard. I want love. He needs release.

I lie underneath.

2   Waiting for his arrival. It is a secret, his presence, all that's inviolable in me. He is zabaglione, sweet with civilisation. I want the pleasure to last, of knowing he'll be here. In the same city. Accessible.

1   His arms are leaden weights around me. He tries to comfort though it pains him. We are at truce, he brings me cups of tea. In the evening, by the window flushed with cascading autumn foliage, he takes sullen sips of wine. I cry from wounds the steaming tannin scours.

2   His viola is often with me. Light, insouciantly decadent, it trickles through me, pouring out in a smile. In the sleepless hours, the suburban hum of fridge and motorcar smooth as nocturnal surf in my ear, I open the case. Black leather frayed near the catch. Inside, the worn red felt. I play a ponderous cello.

1   I am suspicious. He must loathe me. And I loathe his pale fire, a dry ice that burns at a touch. I withdraw, determined to find a meaning outside him.

2   The tan bark outside Llewellyn Hall is slick and sharp underfoot. Tiny native plants bend with the driving rain; the giant concrete walls are streaked and steaming. The lights within glow as from a royal cave. I imagine him by my side, discoursing on Telemann, Monteverdi, opera buffa.

I breathe in the warmth from a damp wool coat. Giddy, I climb to the top of the gallery, where seats are cheap and the sound is best.

1   He wants to split, he says. We stand at the window, bleak of

foliage; winter lights and winter stars dazzling shards on a void. I nod, realising it is so. The tears dry on my cheek, salt sharp. Suddenly he looks so beautiful and sad to me.

2   I think of brandy and pheasant as I reach for the phone, marvel at my luck when he answers it. Then flounder, with nothing to say. He apologises for not ringing. He has been sick, he says. He, sick? Embarrassed, I wish he hadn't bothered to make excuses. I tell him I've rung to ask when he's going to play. A pause. He clears his throat. 'I may not be able. This sickness. Last year I had hepatitis . . . I think it's a relapse.'
'Oh, I'm sorry,' I say, suppressing my anger with him for lying.

1/3   The kilos shed off me. My life, it seems, has shrunken to this room, with its looming wardrobe and cereal stickers on the back of the door. And cut-outs of Gonzo and Alfred E Neuman. The room of a son of a friend. I keep the transistor low so as not to wake her through the gyprock wall. I try yoga, meditation, masturbation, valerian tea. At last, when dawn comes, the outline of a pagoda tree stark against an opal sky, I find a kind of peace: the locked case propped against the wardrobe and me lying stunned on the bed.

2   We make arrangements for dinner. 'I'm almost recovered,' he says.

1   I pursue life, what it is to be human, mature, without ties or responsibilities other than those I choose. I am determined. I am free now, my friends tell me. So does he, when he condescends to meet. We are friends now, he tells me. 'Now we can fuck, without the hassles.' He has a point, and I give in. I go to films, meetings, dinner parties, pubs, concerts, art shows. Alone. The nights are filled with sharp adult voices, warm wine and frost. I must be determined, to brave the frost. By ten o'clock in the evening, before the movie ends or the last cup of coffee is drunk, car windows front and back coat with a thick crust of ice. If you go to the movies, you cover the windscreen with newspaper.

2   I rehearse our conversation. I am teaching more than playing, that is true, but I still have ideas about the instrument and have begun to rough out compositions. The students practise on them.

The students like them, and I feel guilty, because I am jealous of their playing. I would like to be playing instead of teaching. He has no need to teach, or if he does, only occasionally. His music, lilting, almost pastoral in effect, begins to sound shallow. I wonder if he is fussy about his socks.

1   Midnight, maybe after, I leave the fire and the company and wind on my scarf and tug on my gloves and march into the darkness with a potful of boiling water. The frost melts in widening circles like portholes on the glass, then slides in great drops on and under the bonnet. I jump in and start the car, bless the heat from the engine. A quick goodnight from my hosts and they rush inside with the empty saucepan and out of the cold. Within blocks the water on the windscreen has frozen. A sheet of opaque ice, pearled as the dawn. I stop the car, leave the engine running, leap out to crack the ice with my fists. It splinters, that's all. I climb behind the wheel and drive with my head out the window.

Dangerous driving this way. I turn a corner and find I'm in his street. Moving on, thinking I am crazy, and hateful, for spying on him like this. But, mercifully, no unfamiliar cars stand in front. And now I am here, it would be spying if I didn't enter. My house, not long ago.

The side door is open, not even latched. As though in the kernel of the cold dark night he is waiting. The glass panels sweat. A light burns in the kitchen. Something propels me now, a sudden swelling of obsession takes over from the first frosty steps, anger or desire or both. The bare bulb in the kitchen kindles beads of light on the frozen glass, gilds the wrinkled leaves of the African violet he has neglected to water. And on the table, two crystal glasses, a gift from me. And next to one, a woman's bag, the colour of wine.

2   The melody is fading.

3   She takes me in her bed, a foam rubber mattress shoved against the cupboard. I cry: she holds me in her arms. 'He isn't worth it,' she says, crooning it to me. 'Am I brilliant?' I ask, stripped utterly bare, thinking of the crumbling black leather, worn red lining, voluptuous cello standing patient in the room next door. 'No,' she answers, with piercing clarity, 'not brilliant.' She pauses to reflect. 'Creative.'

She falls asleep, spreadwing over the mattress. I climb over her legs, holding onto the cupboard, careful not to disturb her. In the room vacated by her son I watch the parched bones of the pagoda tree darken against the morning sky.

At breakfast she expounds. Already, so young, her face is hardened about the jaw, and then I remember she isn't young, I'm not young, though we have started life anew, and that line of resolve round her chin would be scarcely noticeable in a face whose flesh was firm. She butters toast. 'It's their fucking negativity. That's what nearly finished me off,' she confides. 'I would say to him, every fucking week when you think of it (she laughs), Look, do you love me? Should we go on like this? And the bugger would never tell me, one way or another.' She lays her knife on the side of the plate after cutting the toast in four neat squares. 'They want us to make all the decisions for them.'

2   I ring to postpone the dinner. 'No, I'm not well,' I say. 'Nasty winter flu,' I tell him. He laughs. 'When you're better we'll have a nice quiet time. Two convalescents together.'

1   'You don't have to talk to him,' she says.

He stands flooded in winter sunlight at the door. I see him as though from the end of a telescope, as though contemplating a star. His hair, yellower than I remember, floats from his skull like the ruffled hair of a waking child, the prototype of haloes.

'I'm sorry,' he says, but doesn't move.

I feel myself hurtle down the hallway, head down, arms flapping at my side, some burrowing animal groping towards the sun. I cry, and he soothes me with caresses, and I wonder whether it will be right again, but I cannot take his caresses, and I want it to stop.

3   'You have to find a centre,' she says. 'Something inside yourself.' I agree, weaving her words in the concrete cubicle through the student's rasping chords. The sound quivers and finally disappears, rising high to the acoustical ceiling to hover in the air. The student flattens her back against the chair, the bow loose in her hand, leaning on the cello. 'You okay, Maria?' The student loves me, mistakenly. I smile, heedless of tears. Gingerly she raises the bow and plays on.

'You know what happened to me.' My friend states this, but it is a question. She expects me to know yet wants to repeat it. Her sharp voice is quavering, reminding me of the chin. She drinks milk coffee. 'Let me tell you.' How she had left him, finally, because he wouldn't tell her to. And suddenly everything was light and empty: 'I had this peculiar sensation, like I was skiing so fucking fast I wouldn't be able to stop. And the wind was cutting right through me.' She drank a lot, sobered herself up with Panadols and fucked a lot, with anyone willing. She smiles. 'It helped.' But then she found a protector, a friend. He drank with her, the days ran into nights and into days again and she knew it was morning only when it was time to take another Panadol.

'That's enough for today. You did fine,' I say. The student packs up the bow and cello, throws an arm around my shoulder and suggests we go to lunch.

2   Healthy again. His voice flows over the phone. 'Let's see, I'm busy till Thursday. Yes, Thursday. That all right with you?'

'Fine,' I answer, tentatively.

'Hey, wait a minute. Do you have a car?'

'Yeah. This is Canberra.'

'That's my problem,' he laughs, savouring multiple meanings. 'Can you come and get me?'

'Sure. What time?'

'Seven,' he says. 'We'll have an early night,'

3   We dissect men again at breakfast. He was looking for fun, and thought she was. 'Maybe that's unfair,' she says, pausing to reconsider. He cared, but not as a lover. 'A friend,' she repeats. She smiles, pushes the empty cup and plate towards the middle of the table, winds a strand of brown hair (which she once would have lightened) round her weathered finger. I feel cold in the kitchen, its windows facing west, the day overcast. 'We spent days together, drinking, fucking. He taught me a great deal about sex. He could be relaxed, you know, fuck like a woman, over and over. Wasn't stingy, saving it up for the end.' She looks away, her arm on the back of the chair, gazing somewhere under the sink, perhaps at the bottles her son had neglected to take to the tip.

'Anyway I was lonely one morning, feeling especially blue. I was staying in a house with friends, but they had gone away for the weekend, and I paced from one room to the next feeling I would lose myself in the emptiness. Outside the sun was extra bright, one of those days when all the colours are dense. We lived near a playground: swings, slippery dips, seesaws, painted this dense sort of orange. It wasn't far from where he lived, a Saturday morning, maybe six, seven. I decided I needed to see him.' She laughs, it was a long time ago. 'Of course, he was surprised to see me, surprised too that I was upset. And angry. Any dope would have known not to go visiting a man at six thirty in the morning!'

I sigh. The comfort of it. She had surprised him with another woman. She knows what it's like to discover the truth. I lean back in the wooden chair, cross my arms over the soft pads of my chest with something like satisfaction. They're all bastards. A given. Then suddenly I want to double over, to squeeze out the pain.

'So I went back to the big empty house on Sutter Street, went to their medicine chest and swallowed every sedative and barbiturate in sight. They found me on the swing god knows how many hours later.'

I have heard the story before. How months after she'd left her husband, she had tried to do herself in and nearly succeeded. He, the friend, the protector, had passed on the words of wisdom. 'You have to find a centre.' She could have scrawled it on the walls, emblazoned it on a tee shirt. But I've never heard this part of the story before, how he had come to say it.

'I guess he felt guilty. A little. But more than that he was just plain angry. And, of course, he was right. We had such different expectations of sex those days. Lerv, all that shit.'

She scrapes her chair from the table, stacks her dishes in the sink. Then the forty-year-old bike rider grabs her panniers, lets the wire door slam behind her and heads off in the morning mist for work.

1   He comes in the late afternoon when it's her turn to cook and I lie on the bed in the room with the Alfred E Neumans on the wall and watch the pagoda tree. Blue black limbs, a tangle of eels in the violet sky. He stands by the desk and we mutter words of pain to each other. I stammer, my head turned to the window; he mumbles, shifting the composition sheets on the desk. Then he comes to lie beside me and habit and a strange dark passion, unknown before, take over. The moment he enters everything seems to bleed, even my tears seem streaked with blood.

2   I wait downstairs. There is a clock above the entrance to the corridor that leads to the library, the meetings room, the formal dining room, the bistro. This, the intellectual heart of Canberra; stuffy,

almost comically proper, all blond woods and oriental carpet. The clock ticks away. Seven, seven-fifteen. I begin to feel silly, sitting alone in the foyer. There is a receptionist and I ask her to ring his number. Her look tells me too well what she is thinking. 'He's expecting me,' I say.

'Now?' he asks. He sounds annoyed. 'But we were to have dinner tomorrow night.'

'I thought tonight.'

'No,' he insists. 'Tomorrow. Thursday.'

'Today is Thursday,' I say.

He comes down to the foyer to take me upstairs. His expression sheepish, he lifts his hands. 'I'm so sorry, I really thought today was Wednesday and tomorrow was Thursday. It's the hours I keep. Last night, or was it this morning?' He smiles. Full lips, white teeth, dimpled cheek. 'I've been practising. Exciting, to be working again after all this sickness. I'm afraid I got carried away.' He stops on the landing, hesitates before speaking. At once I know what he's trying to say. 'You see, it's this student, she's been after me for weeks, keeps asking me to have a go at a score of her father's.' His words have the ease of hastily constructed truths, his handsome face is filmed with sweat. 'I can't get rid of her,' he confides, as we begin climbing again.

He introduces us as she appears from the bedroom. He explains to her that he had forgotten a prior engagement. She looks at me and I know in an instant she hates me. He starts to offer drinks, then realises that because of his condition he has no alcohol in store. He apologises and suggests coffee. The living room has regulation university arm chairs and a coffee table, furniture of the type I've seen in countless offices and lecture theatres. There is a bar refrigerator and a sink. There's a music stand, the viola and some sheets. On the nondescript table sits a bowl of peanuts, the bachelor's concession to home entertainment. For her? For me? From the edge of my eye I see her watching me, sizing up my (now) anorexic frame, baggy pants, floral jacket. I take in that she is tallish, blondish, pudgy still. She is awkward. And I, offered a chair, sit and wonder what sort of power has devised this action replay for me.

He looks at her warily and she returns a conspiratorial gaze. He draws his eyes away and reverts to formal tones. 'I am sorry,' he tells her. 'I don't know how it happened, but I simply made a mistake, with the days.' Her eyes, sullen in a pear-shaped face, fix remorselessly on him. He suggests that she stay and have a drink with us but is confounded, as before, by the lack of supplies and so there is nothing to oil the conversation. After a semblance of social exchange, she announces that it should be she who spends the evening with him, on the grounds that she is young and inexperienced. I am tired, and rise from my chair. Suddenly she is gracious. 'Thank you,' she says, regal, victorious. 'You are very good to take it this way.' And, as if to push her original point further, adds, 'It's because you are older and more sophisticated.'

My reply startles me. It reels up from my unconscious, a secret repository where I have stored Dick Tracy comic strips, Barbara Stanwyck movies, things I thought were stages that I passed through but never touched me. Gangsters machining helicopters on the George Washington Bridge, a pair of dead foxes, glass eyes gleaming, flung across a pair of padded shoulders.

'Honey,' I say, 'you're not doing too bad yourself.'

3 'You're back.' There are a group of them in the kitchen, on their way to a meeting. Their voices move in the room, an even chain of bubbles, a steady energy flow. Apart from anything else, I am starving, having missed out on dinner. I race to the cupboard and gorge myself on peanut butter sandwiches. I sense her watching me, ready to be concerned, alarmed, but she sees me eating and supposes I'm all right. 'Haven't you eaten?' I shake my head, tearing wads of bread with my teeth, gulping them down. 'What happened?' I swallow. 'You wouldn't believe it.' The phone rings. 'I finally got rid of her,' he says, and apologises, again. 'I'm going to the dining room. Will you join me?' She watches, wary, as I nod my head to the phone and slide back into the jacket.

4 We eat in the purple bistro. Big steak, big salad, no wine. He tells me – a form of admission – that he has turned forty. We discuss this for a while, skirting around it. Somehow, for an instant, we feel younger. We have come to the bottom rung of a new ladder, like kids at the next stage of school. Back in his room, unable to assuage my hunger, I chew the peanuts. Whole handfuls as we talk. After the sandwiches I must smell like an elephant. We find, after all, we have little in common. Or perhaps too much. He ventures with music. 'I don't like to talk about music,' I say.

'I love to.'

I see he is disappointed but how can I tell him about the black case, the crumbling leather that comes off in streaks of black dust on my fingers? I picture it against the wardrobe. He knows now that I have difficulties in a relationship. I know now that he has one. A free one. No jealousies, conflicts, that I can detect. He seems open, kind. I can barely talk for the peanuts. They stick to my throat, take forever to swallow. I remember a concert of his I attended. Imagining the music penetrate, closing my eyes for the notes. Everything that music must be, disembodied emotion. Without the viola, he would converse about chords and vibratos. I see the black curls, the smooth complexion, the curve of the collar on his white shirt, the dark eyes. He too seems lost in himself, and I recognise the gulf in experience, perception. We drink instant coffee. We sit in a room with anonymous furniture, white-walled, beige-curtained. There is a faint hum from the air conditioner, no sound of the weather outside. The curtains are drawn, but I know as we talk, or attempt to, that the frost is creeping up my wind-screen: in a poetic flash I imagine it the dust of fallen stars. Suddenly he laughs. 'She wanted me to end her virginity.'

I stare. 'You sound surprised.'

'I am.'

I look at him again.

WHY I LIKE MEN

Edith Speers

mainly i like men because they're different
they're the opposite sex
no matter how much you pretend they're ordinary
human beings you don't really
believe it

they have a whole different language and geography
so they're almost as good
as a trip overseas when life gets dull
and you start looking
for a thrill

next i like men because they're all so different
one from the other
and unpredictable so you can never really know
what will happen from
looks alone

like anyone else i have my own taste with regard
to size and shape and colour
but the kind of style that has nothing to do
with money can make you bet
on an outsider

lastly i guess i like men because they are the other
half of the human race
and you've got to start somewhere
learning to live and let live
with strangers

maybe it's because if you can leave your options open
ready to consider love
with such an out and out foreigner
it makes other people seem
so much easier

LESBIAN HEAVEN

Dawn Cohen

They say there's a Lesbian heaven
You go to when you are dead,
On arrival you're given a chlorophyll juice,
and a customary double bed.

You live in communal delight
And bliss is the life and the way,
Which should come as no surprise,
cos the women make love all day.

Virginia Woolf holds parties,
makes eyes at Sackville-West,
Radclyffe Hall stands by,
in a suit and a tie
looking her dykish best.

Pankhurst is no longer a classist,
and Queen Victoria knows how it's done,
and you can tell,
by the glint in her eye
that she also knows that it's fun.

Everything has a flavour,
and you can hear the sound of colour,
and nobody has a halo
that's brighter than any other.

There are Lesbian trees
and a Lesbian breeze,
a Lesbian moon at night
Lesbian lakes and Lesbian seas
That sparkle in Lesbian light

They say there's a Lesbian heaven
You go to when you are dead
but we shouldn't have to die for it
So let's make it here instead.

THE WOMAN IN THE MOON

Rosemary Jones

She was dream/she was honey/she was soft.

I fell for the eyes first, it was the eyes, then the lips, then the eyebrows, the way she'd raise one once, then the other. In-quisitive. Sceptical, but not high brow. In-quisitive.

She was dream/she was honey/she was tough.

She used to drive me around. I talked, she drove. I watched. I loved the way she sat behind the wheel and when we'd park in the street she'd put her hand on the back of the passenger seat. I was the passenger, and she'd manoeuvre, one hand on the wheel. She could do a lot one-handed.

I'd watch as she looked over and above, just above my face and through the back window as she edged into a parking space. I'd watch and my heart sank, she made my heart sink and then float upwards, skywards, oh, she was dream.

She was tough, she could wield an axe and drive a bus and throw an anchor and ride a horse and cook French gourmet or stuff ducklings, she could have chopped their heads off if she had to. She would have been good on an excavation site, in a hurricane, in floods or navigating by night.

She was dream/she was honey/she was sad. She was often sad, sad but brusque with tears, she had no time for tears, I never heard her sob, she couldn't come out with a wracking sob if she tried/she was dreaming/she was tough, she had dreams. They were tough too and full of tears, images of tears, dreamt tears like little crystals, refractions of tears lingering in the background, always lingering as if someone rose up from in front of her eyes and waved a coloured scarf at her, an eclipse of red or crimson, some colour she didn't like to admit to and couldn't take on. There was a colour somewhere inside her she couldn't take on, she didn't try, she tried not to remember the colour, she waved it away with her hand, a gesture of brief defiance . . .

She was dream/she was colour/she was love, she made love in defiance of one colour and in celebration of all others. She pressed the red, or was it crimson she pressed back like pushing someone's hair from their forehead, gently, firmly, she wouldn't see the colour, it made her shiver. If she did see it she shivered. I could feel it – shiver, shiver, little burning bits, she was luminous at her edge, she was luminous wrestling with colour, the colour she swore she did not see, the colour she dismissed like some high falutin lady dismissing a waiter. And she'd stay with the soft pastels and the rigorous night blues and slices of silver and never dare to come full bore at the reds and the crimsons or the plum, the strong plum stain, she never came at that . . .

She was dream/she was silver/she was tough/she was crying . . . crying like an orphan at a party for lost love and lost souls as if she'd gathered them all up in her arms without a murmur, without giving anything away, she was crying/I saw her/I watched her crying and came out from the trees and into her reflection to tell her she could cry, I didn't mind if she cried/I wanted her to cry because she was dreaming/she was crying like a moon. I wanted to tell her there was a beginning, tears could make a beginning, together we could make a beginning.

She was strange-eyed and soft hearted. Eyes like saucers and a heart like, a heart like something fallen from out of the moon.

And she made love like a dancer/she danced love with lithe fingers, she danced it and sang it, did the splits for love/she did pirouettes for love/she loved like a dancer/she made love like a piece of moon which dropped away from her and into me. She made love but the sun got in her eyes, the colour crimson got in her saucer-like eyes/she was all eyes, eyes like saucers and the sun got in her eyes, the colour sheered off from the sun and slanted into her eyes . . .

She was dreaming, she said, she was dreaming of love . . .

She was wet like roses in winter, petals full of dew, she was wet but the sun caught at her eyes, stung her eyes/she was wet like the lips of petals on a very winter morning but the sun/something crimson/she was crying and I held her as if I was driving and holding the back of the passenger seat manoeuvring into a space.

And I was crying/I saw the sun at her eyes and I squinted/I couldn't help myself, the sun had come into my eyes/she was wide-eyed, crater-wide, crying as if she saw crimson and red and orange and plum/she was crying and I squinted – too long. I couldn't help myself . . .

There was the sun, in my eyes, and I saw the crimson and red and the sharp shriek of plum, and I saw her wide eyes soft as water as I let them fall on me like the strange rays at dusk when she rises. I lit up like a beacon and felt her fall, soft thud against me, full of loss, full of hope, full of night love . . .

And I lost her. She was dream/she was honey/she was soft.

She was dream/she was silver/she was tough. I lost her silver, to the sun.

FRAGMENT

Gillian Hanscombe

. . . so I bowed and nodded as best I could (though not as well as you) and loved the people for loving you and admired the people for admiring you and now and again I sensed you tease or tarry or find something someone said just useful enough to keep and I was (if you'll allow) so proud of you and pleased . . .

. . . and when we got back to whatever bed we were sharing then, wherever it was, and were undressing ourselves (and each other – it is the same) then one of us said to the other
—well how did we do? sideways, that is? were we all right?
—yes my darling we were all right, said the other;
—but now let us see how we do face to face . . .

. . . it was always odd (wasn't it?) how there was no after-wards . . . the signs were there: the sweating, the racing of hearts, the heat . . . and we were tired, inevitably . . . but it never actually stopped; there was always a tongue somewhere on an eyebrow or cheek, a hand somewhere, or arms that curved, legs that got muddled; always the climbing or riding or scudding or falling; always the yes saying yes and yes . . .

. . . and sometimes there was the wondering about who was who . . .

Red as a Beetroot

Helen Pausacker

I go into the greengrocers' to buy vegetables . . . carrots, spinach, tomatoes – whatever is in season. I'm a vegetarian, so I eat a lot of vegetables. Sometimes when I'm having people to dinner, I like to buy a couple of avocados or something else that I wouldn't buy normally. This always bothers the greengrocerwoman.

'They're a dollar fifty each,' Sophia says.

'That's fine. I'm having people to dinner tonight.'

They've known me since I was unemployed and watching every cent. When I got my first job a couple of years ago, Sophia gave me a kiss and Franz gave me an apple. Often when I go in we chat for half an hour. They are German Jews who emigrated at the beginning of the Nazi regime. We talk about their past life, their family and what I am doing, my family and what I am cooking for dinner. Sophia always wants to know how many people are coming to dinner and what I am serving them.

But when the woman is there, I just want to run out of the shop. I don't know her name, but she sits there often, on the chair beside the counter, with her legs astride. She's probably in her early fifties, with short, dark, curly hair. She's a big woman – not fat or chubby, but she takes up a space in the shop that no one else seems to. I think she must do shift work, because she's often there at half-past four. But sometimes she'll stay for an hour, talking to Sophia and Franz. She's got a loud, booming voice. You can't ignore her. And she looks at me when I walk into the shop in a way that says she knows what I'd look like without my clothes on. I always blush. I feel exposed in front of Sophia and Franz. Not that they've ever said anything or looked disapprovingly.

One day she says to me, 'And what are you cooking for dinner tonight?' Sophia can ask me that. She's my greengrocer, and it's her business. But it's none of this woman's business.

But I tell her. 'I'm cooking mushroom soup and cheese soufflé.'

'Oh,' she says, 'fancy stuff, huh? Well, in that case, I won't invite you to dinner. I cook plain food myself.'

I turn beetroot red. What am I meant to reply to that? I feel like a fourteen-year-old schoolgirl, blushing when a boy talks to her on the tram. I've given up all that stuff. I decided a year ago, when I turned twenty, that I was going to be a radical celibate. I've enjoyed this year, living on my own and having friends to dinner. It's been quiet.

This woman is playing havoc with my whole body. Just the way she looks at me. It's like a man . . . well, maybe not. Men don't worry whether you're responding to them. She does. And I am responding, and she knows it. That's the problem. And do I *want* to have dinner with her? Was she offering me dinner with her, or just teasing? I'm too red to think.

I mutter something incoherent and rush from the shop.

On the footpath I stop and think, Maybe she wanted *me* to ask *her* to dinner. Maybe she's just lonely.

Maybe I'm lonely. But I try not to think about that. I can't go back in anyway. Maybe another time.

Maybe never.

It's the day before christmas, and the greengrocers are going to close shop for ten days. They're going to visit their daughter, who lives in New Zealand, Sophia informs me.

The woman is sitting there. It's the first time I've seen her since she asked, or rather, didn't ask me to dinner. She catches my eye when I walk in. I realise I was wrong about her just being lonely. She might be lonely, but she also knows something about me that I don't want her to know.

She watches me as I come in and my walk gets all self-conscious. I love the attention, and I hate it at the same time. I can't relax, can't stand normally, can't concentrate on the conversation with Sophia, but I pretend to ignore the woman.

'I'm not going away,' I tell Sophia, 'I'm having christmas dinner at my mother's. And my sister's coming over from Adelaide. She'll be staying at my place for four days.'

Another customer comes in, and Sophia kisses me on both

cheeks, and gives me a big hug. 'Have a happy holiday,' she says, as she comes round to give me my box of fruit and vegies. 'And here's a bag of grapes. We're not going to sell them all, they'll only go off.'

Franz looks at Sophia. 'Can I kiss her too?' he asks. Then he remarks jovially to me, 'Don't want the old girl to get jealous!' He doesn't ask me if I want to kiss him, but I don't mind, because he reminds me of my grandfather. I put my cheek over the counter for him.

Then I quickly grab up my bags and call out, 'Have a happy holiday' to the woman, and run away before she decides that she'll kiss me too.

Maybe she wasn't going to try. Maybe I would have felt worse if she hadn't tried. I'm glad I didn't hang around to find out.

The years go by and my celibacy fades. I get busier and often buy fruit and vegies at the milkbar. So I hardly see the woman in the greengrocers'.

My girlfriend's been nagging me to get my ear pierced. 'An earring would look so nice against your dark hair,' she says.

I mention it to the other waitresses at work and one of them offers to take me the next day. 'You shouldn't stop and think about it,' she says. 'I'll get a couple more holes done in my ears while we're at it.'

The next time I go to the greengrocers' the woman is sitting there. She takes me in with one glance.

'Hm,' she says, 'You've had your ear pierced? Just one?'

I look her in the eye for the first time and smile.

'Yes,' I reply.

ULULATION FOR A RED HEADED WOMAN

Donna McSkimming

for Julia

if you kiss a red head lick her ears & you'll
hear crimson semitones; the sacred fires lit
& attracting revellers to some dark hill
& dancing, dancing till you fall exhausted
against the old tree shivers/remembers bonfires.

or

if you kiss a red head stroke her hair,
like silk snapping electric. static.
imbedding spark on spark, till the future
detonates along the ley lines of your palms.

or

if you kiss a red head, taste her nipples
translucent & touched lilac – as the core
of the flame – as the space between the
Goddess's breaths. a helix from nipple to;
eyes begin a canticle in blue a scale sliding
finding the spiral through the centre
of an iridescent iris

or

if you kiss a red head like running downhill
through acres of opium poppies. the petals
stinging a skinful of pungent kisses. & poppy
heads – knuckles into flesh already
begging/bursting full. O grip the inner thigh hard
& let the opiates roll like balm across my
stomach.

or

if you kiss a red head & the moon slips
from the dark to be passed a garnet from
tongue to tongue & pitched past point
of; the axis shifts & blood flames into
an aria burning pure blue. you'll know
fire as a high note. woman & pitch exalted.

MURIEL AND THE TIGER

Kaye Moseley

It was there again. Muriel looked away from the window. The lilacs and the lace on the window-sill hung suspended like shattered stalactites. Behind them she sensed the tiger.

'Your cigarette is about to burn the carpet,' she remarks. I stop typing and pick up my ciggy.

'You smoke too much,' she tells me in her disapproving voice.

I know, I know. I don't want to think about it. Sometimes I think she is my conscience incarnated.

'They'll get you in the end,' she says.

Not a warning, a statement of fact. If I listen to her I betray myself. I am captivated. But she's supposed to be my muse.

Get off your rose and inspire me.

She appeared in my room just over a month ago, when I was lying on my bed watching the cigarette smoke waft to the black ceiling, geni-type figures floating and stretching across the space and there she was. She thinks black ceilings are her thing, she stands out so well. She's been here ever since.

I have read to her Shakespeare's sonnets. She has a liking for the Elizabethan. But she said my voice was a drone.

'Uplift yourself!'

I, however, am not made of vaporous essence and cannot float around ceilings.

She continued regardless. 'Ah, she was so interesting! So filled with the *joie de vivre!* We had a sympatico relationship, so close! But she was a dreadful stay-at-home. I never could entice her to leave that mousehole.' My muse has travelled.

After a while I give up trying to write. Muriel is in the kitchen aware of the tiger like a film that has gone from slow motion to a pause. I cannot handle two frames of thought at the same time. Her voice mesmerises me and I forget to listen to myself. Much easier to move the typewriter over and doodle. I draw clouds. They are akin to her. I can catch her wisps, the faint trace of melancholy. She has lived so long. You cannot always be indifferent.

She comes from the long ago of everyone's dreamtime. She has a ruby in her navel and cornflowers in her hair, and her eyes are rimmed in dusky brown. She bears the scent of fields and sun. She is still young. She was worshipped in the long ago. My cat worships her.

Drifting, drifting. Back to the drawing board. Blueprint for a revolution. The ants are invading my house. I'll have to stand the honey in a bowl of water. But even then they swim across. They're also in the fridge. Crawling across the typewriter, even my study is not safe. I think about mortein. My mother sprayed the house with mortein all through my childhood.

'They're poisoning your world,' she says. 'The enzymes, you know, in your stomach and nervous system.'

No, I don't know, and don't tell me anymore. I don't think I'd like knowing.

'The women used to grow mint around the porches. They spread it over the matting, with yarrow and tansy. Such fragrance!'

What women?

'The Mothers. I think they forgot about the insects in the end. They liked the freshness so much.'

I make a mental note to raid the garden for what little sprigs of mint are there. The garden reminds me of Muriel and the tiger. I pull the typewriter back.

The days were quiet. The air was balmier, warmer. She felt winter dispersing, clinging in dark corners, but ineffectual. The radio played all day. Muriel sat down to consider the situation.

She had read a little about insanity. But it was really a clinical term and she had never understood exactly what it meant. She supposed the tiger could be a hallucination. But then, the last time, she was aware of it before she saw it. The hairs on the nape of her neck had tingled. Something had compelled her to look out of the window. And there it was, sitting among the lilacs. The yellow eyes had stared at her.

'She must know the tiger is herself,' she says.

No, she doesn't. She thinks it is external.

'Like you and my snakes,' she says.

Yes, like me and her snakes. They unnerved me at first, being a city girl at heart. I thought they were reflections in my specs. The glass has a way of picking up the light and distorting it into shapes. And, besides, you just don't expect to find a snake in your study. I didn't even know what brand it was. They're all venomous to me. But it was semi-transparent. It came with her. There's always one sort or another sliding around her.

'They burned my flowers to keep them away,' she says.

Who?

'The Romans, of course. Such a giggle, they were! And so scared of my pets!' She is scornful. I know she didn't favour the Romans much.

'They were great ones for categorising,' she says, 'and for belittling what was once held to be great.'

She has a slightly higher regard for the Greeks but more so for the Cretans. Greece, she tells me, had a vamped culture. They weren't a scratch on the Cretans. The little I know about Crete I learned when I studied western art. I remember the murals of the bull vaulting and of the dolphins in the palace at Knossos, the big urns with their marine designs of octopus and fish, and the Snake-goddess.

I stare at my muse thoughtfully. I hadn't made the connection before. She has a slight smile on her lips.

The Greeks, did they worship your snakes?

'The Greeks had a healthy respect for the serpentine,' she says. I have a mental flash of the Greek goddess Athena, overwhelmingly tall and clad in armour.

'She was a Mother,' says my muse. 'She was worshipped as such long before the Greeks. *They* tried to make her a goddess of war. Pah!'

I seem to recall reading somewhere that Athena was the daughter of Zeus.

'Not so!' she flashes angrily. 'Zeus was an interloper. He belonged to the Dorians. They brought him with them from the north. He had no roots in Greece. And he was impotent anyway. They fabricated his fatherhood. Said Athena sprang from his head! A thought-form indeed!'

I think I have touched a hornet's nest. I say no more, but decide to visit my local library and do a bit of quick reading. We sit in silence until I feel her anger dissipating. I return to Muriel and my typewriter.

Muriel did not tell Jack about the tiger, not this time. Last time she had had to endure his jokes for weeks. He told all his friends that she must be smoking pot on the sly. They all thought it was funny. On the day of the firm's annual picnic they cracked jokes about tigers all day. Muriel had felt humiliated. This time she maintained silence, and this time the tiger's presence was stronger. At night when she lay in bed she could feel its power growing.

'There aren't many of them left, you know,' she says.

What?

'Tigers. Less than four thousand. Your time has killed them. Once they were mighty beasts in spirit and number.'

I stop tapping and reflect on this piece of information. It seems sometimes that I travel in circles, invariably returning to a dying planet. This is not good for the creative spirit. It depresses me. I shove off the thought and type again.

It was Thursday. Muriel always dreaded Thursdays. Jack went to the pub with his mates when they knocked off work, and he always came home drunk. Oh, he drank a lot anyway, but he celebrated pay-day with a vengeance. Muriel was sometimes sick with fear.

He was different when he was drunk. Sort of mean and nasty, always looking for a fight. It was like living with two different people. One would leave in the morning and the other one would come home at night.

She had taken to cooking a casserole on Thursdays because she never knew how late he'd be and she could keep adding water to it so it wouldn't dry out. He would abuse her if his dinner was burned. But sometimes he wouldn't eat it anyway. He'd sit in front of the television with a can instead. Muriel would sit in the kitchen and do the daily crossword. It helped to occupy her mind.

I go to the lounge-room and pour myself a small glass of port. Muriel's discomfort makes me uncomfortable. How can you live with someone for so long when you have so little communication? I return to the study with my port and light a cigarette. My muse is sitting on top of the cabinet with her eyes closed.

'They were great ones for wine,' she says.

Who?

'The Zeus people. They sacrificed with flesh and wine to him. Athena said they were barbarians.'

I sip my port slowly. Surely sacrifices were also made to Athena?

'Fruit and grain with milk and honey. Athena did not allow the spilling of blood.'

One day I'll write a book about all of this. It's growing on me, a vine creeping all over my mind. I untangle the threads and find Muriel.

Muriel began preparing the dinner. She cut the meat up and added it to the fried onions. Normally she would pick a few herbs from her garden to add to it, but the tiger was there. She used dried oregano instead. She worked methodically without really thinking. All her senses were gone. She almost felt like she wasn't even in the kitchen.

Three o'clock. A great gust of wind hit the window. A north wind, warm and dry.

The phone rings. I go into the lounge-room and talk for a while. My muse drifts through to the kitchen. My cat follows her. Thick as thieves, those two. I hang up and follow them both to the kitchen to make some coffee.

She is floating above the window. My cat sits watching her with wide adoring yellow eyes. I sit down and light a cigarette. If I were Muriel, what would I do? My muse watches me.

'There was a time,' she says, 'when I walked alone in pride and strength. I gave to the Mothers the wild grains, the wild cows and the mountain goats, and they tamed them. They made earthenware pots and baked the ground grain and spun wool and wove it. They named me mistress of all living things. I gave them reeds and they made music in my honour. They built shrines for my worship.

'Later, their sons married me to Zeus and made him my lord and master. Now they worship Zeus in my temples. But I am of an older power.'

I put out my cigarette and smile at her. So.

Muriel looked up, into the wide yellow eyes. For one moment she was frozen with fear, and then it went. She smiled, opened the window and let the tiger in.

When Jack came home Muriel was gone. The kitchen was empty, and the lace curtains fluttered aimlessly through the window.

PATERNITY SUIT

Marion Halligan

Two young men sitting sunk deep into ancient grey armchairs like concave hippopotamuses. Drinking beer out of cans. In a house enveloped in large old foreign trees keeping out the hot summer. Smelling as it always used of coffee and garlic, and now in summer of plums. (Plums the boon of neglected gardens, not needing attention in order to fruit.) And soot. All winter the Rayburn burns; enough hours of the day and night there is somebody awake in the house to stoke it, and never does this faint stench of long-burned wood depart.

Gerry sits in a hippopotamus chair and sometimes makes conversation with Don, and thinks that it is good to be back in this house, almost as good as having left it. He snuffs up the smells of soot and plums and coffee and garlic and a certain human mustiness with nostalgia and thinks of his own new bare painted woody flat. Don goes out to the fridge and brings back two more cans.

– Not sorry you moved out?

– No, no; well, not mostly, adds politeness. It was great; but, well, it's good to be on your own. Your own boss, you know?

– Yeah, says Don. I s'pose.

Sybil wanders in with a handful of plums and goes and gets a can of beer to join them. She sits in the doorway, on the floor leaning against the lintel, and walks her bare dirty feet up the opposite side. She takes out a packet of Drum and rolls a skinny clumsy cigarette, perhaps with marijuana, and the complex manipulation of the three processes, the drawing on the cigarette (and blowing out the smoke and staring at the exhalation in case it were meaningful), the chewing of the plums, and the pulling at the beer can, takes all her attention. Her mass of frizzy hair is like a pillow softening the lintel to her head. Sucking at the cigarette, the plums, the beer, she makes no conversation.

She is wearing dungarees and no shirt, and when she moves, walking her bare feet up the opposite lintel, sometimes the bib on the dungarees moves too and shows her tiny breasts rubbed pink by the coarse fabric, and Gerry feels slightly excited, but by remembrance of sexuality rather than the desire to renew it, the faint shameful excited memory of lust rather than its renascence. He wishes she'd go away, so he could go on talking or not to Don without needing to take this self-absorbed figure in the doorway into some polite account.

When Gerry had graduated with quite a decent economics degree and got his job in the public service, he'd been happy for a while to go on living in the house which had sheltered much of his undergraduate career. But had gradually become ambitious, and finally decided, with accumulating money, to move out and take a flat on his own. The house, in Braddon, was a rather battered government place but old enough to be spacious, and the garden was old too and rather a wilderness, but keeping the house cool and producing the plums, and vegetables if anybody planted them, and apples that might have been all right if they had been sprayed against codlin moth. He'd enjoyed his years of living there but felt like trying out on his own. Sybil was happy to move in and take his place.

He met her again at a party in the same suburb several months later. She was as thin and brown as ever, her grey eyes as large, her hair a grey bonnet about her bony face, frizzy and dull. She was wearing a pale green kimono tied round the waist with a long purple silk scarf and no shoes. Do you like this kimono? she said. It belonged to a lady of the Japanese court. It's a hundred and thirty years old. It was a rather boring party and he was pleased to see her; they talked for a while and she invited him home for a cup of tea. The house was around the corner and the idea more attractive than the party.

She made jasmine tea and they sat on the sofa in the empty Saturday night house and she stared at him with her large eyes and asked him did he mind very much being a public servant. He was trying to answer this question honestly when she knelt on the sofa to reach across for the packet of Drum on the table beside him. The kimono, which was held together only by the slippery silk scarf, gaped open and he saw her small hard breast, hardly larger than its nipple. He put out his hand without thinking to see if it was as hard and pointed as it looked and then she was sitting over his lap and the purple scarf had undone and the kimono fallen back and she was naked and they were making love.

It was the first time with a girl he didn't think he was in love with. Always before it had been the climax of a plot of passion, of a long desiring. Or short. But existing. Here it was just friendly, like a conversation. Except that she was more rude than he would have been with the most casual of guests; afterwards she told him quite angrily to go home. She hated people to stay with her. A week later he called and invited her to dine expensively with him; she came wearing the same ancient beautiful kimono and high-heeled sandals this time. They went to bed again afterwards, but she intimidated him a bit, and he did not want to see her again very soon.

This Sunday morning he is on his way home from Mackay's hardware shop where he's been buying brackets to put up shelves; he is getting quite houseproud in his small flat. He's called on the offchance of seeing some of the old gang, and is pleased to find Don, less so with Sybil.

– Come again soon, says Don when he leaves, and he does a month or so later, with a few cold tins in the Esky and the excuse of a trip to Mackay's to buy a new garbage bin. Don is there, and Mark, and a new bloke called Sim, but no girls; Sybil's got a job as a barmaid on Sundays and Janet's away for the weekend. The beer goes down well, and he decides to have a party at the flat and ask all his friends.

– Great idea, says Mark. You must be fucking lonely way out there on your own.

– Well, Mawson's not the end of the earth, you know, he says.

– Yeah, but it's not Braddon, is it? You're not here at the centre of the fucking universe. He chews up some bread and cheese and rides off on his bike to the library.

– True, says Don. You must be lonely.

Sim says, No girls in the house, and tries to leer but only manages a shy smile.

– I've never noticed them being much good to anyone, says Gerry. I mean they don't do much housework and they don't sleep with you, so what's the point?

– Oh, I wouldn't be too sure of that, says Sim. Sybil's all right.

It has occurred to Gerry that he is not a particularly energetic man. He plays a game of squash now and then to stop the beer getting to his gut, but he can't be bothered with weekend sport any more, the cricket and football of the old uni days. A few of the blokes at work are into windsurfing, but that seems a lot of effort. He bummed around a bit when he was a student, took a year or so off and went up north, did some surfing, saw a bit of the country. Now his job keeps him pretty busy. And mucking about the flat. Pot plants and a patch of garden. A lot of reading. Evenings with a glass or two of red and an increasing variety of decent books. He takes girls out now and then but hasn't found anybody really amazing yet. Nobody to live with, nobody he'd want about all the time. He's beginning to wonder if he is becoming a confirmed bachelor. He gets into the habit of dropping into the Braddon house on Sundays, there's usually company. One or other of the old gang, mostly not Sybil because of barmaiding. Sometimes Janet, a tall strong girl who can't decide whether she wants to go on and finish her degree or become a gardener; she works casually at the latter (as she has at the former) and likes it; she thinks it would probably be a more profitable career than any produced by a redundant history degree.

They sit and talk and drink beer or white wine and discuss such things, Gerry trying not to show the smugness of a decent job and prospects; he knows that with the right kind of ambition and attitude plus some clever but not difficult manipulation he can rise. Sim despises this as establishment; he is proud of having dropped out of law a year ago. Now he busks in Civic and is trying to get a rock group going (look at Pete Garrett); the others have forbidden him to do it in their house. Don is twenty-one and will graduate in economics soon too; he doesn't know whether to despise or admire Gerry's luck.

– What about Sybil? asks Gerry. She must be just about ready to finish, mustn't she? She's been around for years.

Don guffaws. She'll be lucky to make it inside the nine-year limit, the way she's going. She's been at it for five without a lot to show.

– Especially now, says Janet, with this bee she's got in her bonnet.

– That's what you call it, is it? says Don. My mother always said bun in the oven.

– Ha ha, says Janet. I don't mean the fact, I mean what she's doing about it.

Gerry thinks he knows what this conversation is about but can't quite believe it.

Sim says, What *is* she doing about it?

– Nothing. That's the point. She's going to have it.

– Do I gather from this that Sybil is pregnant? asks Gerry.

– You do. You do, says Don. God she's mad. Abortion's so easy these days. She's mad not to have one.

– Well, Sybil knows that, that it's easy I mean. She's done it before. No, she wants to have a baby. She likes the idea of bringing up a child. And she thinks she is a good age–or rather, she thinks she's getting on a bit and better late than never. At twenty-four. Janet grins. She doesn't want to wait until she's a geriatric like me.

– Who's the father? asks Gerry, instantly regretting the baldness of the question.

– Who knows, with Sybil, says Don.

– Is she that promiscuous, says Gerry.

– Oh, I dunno. In a kind of way. She has relationships, you know, with odd people. A while ago it was a bricklayer she met on a building site at uni, and she did nothing but rave on about the realness of working with your body and all that crap; she's always getting terrifically intense about some weird guy or other, but you never know what's in it.

– Perhaps he's the father, says Gerry.

– Maybe. Haven't seen him around for a while, though. Anyway, it's not me, that's for certain.

– Nor me, says Sim. Not this time.

– Well, I expect you'll find out sooner or later, says Gerry. I mean, won't she get married to him?

All three look at him in amazement. Bloody hell, no, says Janet. This is Sybil's baby, all her own work. The last thing she wants is a husband.

– Wouldn't be economical, anyway, says Sim. This way she gets a supporting mother's pension and can live off the state for the next twenty years or so–if it goes to uni and all that. Sim is an expert on all forms of state aid.

Gerry in his later incarnation of tax-paying civil servant is a bit shocked by this but wise enough not to show it in this company. Instead he says, very casual, When's it due?

The two men roll up their eyes and twist down their mouths to indicate they have nothing to do with such information.

Janet says, I dunno. About six months, I suppose.

Don looks at Gerry. You're helluva interested, Gerry, my son. It wouldn't be anything to do with you, would it?

– Shit no. Why should it be anything to do with me? It's just interesting, that's all.

Gerry is more than interested. He's doing sums and wishes that he had some accurate figures. It's about three months ago that he went with Sybil. The baby's due in about six months. That certainly adds up to about nine months. It's not conclusive, of course. Not with such vague dates. Talk of supporting mothers' pensions has made him think of supporting fathers; what if she claims paternity, makes him pay? Sybil strikes him as a bit of a slut; he thinks of the slippery kimono and instant nakedness, of the large pink-rubbed nipples uncovered by the stiff bib of her dungarees, remembers that first night and how easy she was, practised. She could have been sleeping with half a dozen men at the same time.

But if she says she wasn't? Claims him as father? He looks about his flat, at the oriental rug he's just bought, his leather chair; after so many years as a poor student he's just beginning to enjoy the fruits of a regular income, two years now, and money coming in comfortably and just a little mounting up. He doesn't want to have to support a child almost certainly not his. And if he refuses? A scandal? A court case? That won't do the promising career much good. And will be expensive, apart from anything. Sybil's parents are on a posting in Japan, but there are doubtless powerful friends. The best of lawyers.

He goes to the pub where she works and tries to catch her coming off duty. He's not soon successful; the first time she looks at him, says, Hello stranger, and disappears out the back. But eventually she agrees to have a drink with him.

They sit in a gaudy bar and he makes several bumbling remarks which she just looks at with mocking eyes. She has taken out her Drum packet and is making one of her skinny cigarettes.

– Should you be doing that? he says.

– Why the fuck not? She holds the cigarette between her first two fingers and picks shreds of tobacco off her tongue with her thumb and third finger. It's a gesture he hates. The smoke winds up past her squinting eyes and entwines itself in the frizz of her hair. It seems to him that this might be why it is so dull.

– I thought . . . he says, but she stares at him and he stops.

– How are you, anyway? he goes on. You're looking very well.

And indeed she is. She paints her face for the job and makes it beautiful, her mouth soft and peach-like, her eyes huge and dark-fringed; there's nothing left of the sharp and peaky look that makes her resemble a decadent waif. Even the dull cloud of her hair could be a tarnished halo.

– Oh, I feel good, she says. She claps her hands across her breasts. And my boobs are swelling.

She doesn't know when the baby is due. Didn't the doctor tell her? No, she hasn't been. Why should she? Having babies is natural. On one of his visits to Dalton's (he regularly checks out the bookshops) he finds himself buying a book about pregnancy. He calls at the Braddon house. Brought you a present, he says. Ha ha. She refuses to look at it. Couldn't care less about the table for calculating birth dates. She's not interested in such mechanical matters. So he leaves it with her.

The next time he calls he is almost run over by a guy dressed in leather and metal studs speeding out of the driveway on a motorbike. Sybil is wandering about the house wearing nothing but a very thin Indian shift; not just the large brown nipples on the newly swelling breasts are visible but the pale fuzz of her pubic hair as well. He is a bit excited but more enraged.

– What do you want, Gerry, she says, her hands on her hips pulling the thin shift tight. Do you want to screw?

– If you like, he says, desperately casual.

– Well, I don't, not now, thanks, she says, mocking him.

– That the father I just saw leaving? he says.

– Wouldn't you like to know!

– Wouldn't you?

– Very funny. I don't know why you're so interested in this baby, Gerry. Let me tell you something. This my baby, it's not anyone else's. No one else is going to have anything else to do with it.

– Oh well, I expect it was an immaculate conception. Or maybe Zeus in the shape of a motorbike.

She picks up the pregnancy book and throws it at him. He catches it.

– One thing, Gerry, *you* certainly didn't have anything to do with it. Nothing at all. You're the last person I'd choose for a sperm bank.

This is the news he's been waiting for. This is the great weight off his chest. Sybil claims in the most positive terms that he isn't her baby's father, and this is what counts. He won't have to pay, there won't be a scandal. He's found out what he wanted to know.

He doesn't feel very elated. but that isn't surprising. It was a nasty scene. Sybil is almost certainly a slut, and she's not very good-natured either. Not at all the sort of person to be mixed up with.

He's still holding the book that he caught. (The old cricketer's reflexes still on the ball.) Walking down the drive he wiffles through it, thinking wryly this is one book I haven't got any use for any more. There's a slip of paper in it; it's one of those paperbacks that don't open properly and it's caught firmly, that's why it didn't fly out when Sybil threw it. By now he's in the car and looks at the figures on the paper. He laughs out loud and tosses it on the seat beside him. It's another victory. Sybil succumbed. She couldn't resist calculating the dates after all.

Gerry can't resist either. Now he's got the precise figures he needed; the date of the last period. But he doesn't want to calculate ahead to the birth, but back to the moment of conception. He goes through his diary to find the date of the dull party. It's spot on in the fertile period.

There's no doubt at all; Gerry could be the father of Sybil's baby. Not certainly since he doesn't know whether she slept with anybody else in the same period but, even if she did, there is still a quite high chance that the child is his. Well, it's all merely curiosity value now, since Sybil has waived all claims. I should have had a tape-recorder along, he thinks. But he feels safe enough. She seemed to mean it.

Why then does he call in to the hotel the next three Sundays? The first two weeks he gets nothing but commercial chit-chat; she wreathes away behind the busy bar like a will-o-the-wisp, the foolish fire, and the dull stiff smoke of her hair mocks him. On the third she has a black eye. She puts as much insolence as possible into the remaining one.

– Ran into a door. What else?

– The macho type with the bike, wasn't it?

He is upset. The pretty peach mouth, the one eye large and anxiously insolent, the sad powerless slit of the other, make him feel wobbly inside. Too much beer probably. Though he can't help the sneaking thought that maybe it might be what is meant by bowels yearning. This awful sick churning feeling inside. He feels all biblical.

– Let me take you home, he says, and this time she doesn't flit off willy-wispy, she stays and lets him take her home.

She makes lemon verbena tea. He stares into the cup for a fortune, a future.
– Sybil, why don't we get married?

Surprised, she is silent for a minute.

–No, she says.

I'm mad, he thinks. I don't want to marry Sybil. I don't like her. I'm not even in love with her. I'm out of my tiny mind. Bloody lucky she said no. Could be stuck with going through with it.

He asks her a number of times. Cajoles. Begs. Pleads. Explains. Always she says no. Sometimes with reasons. She doesn't want a husband, she is perfectly happy on her own, it's her baby, that's it.

– It's not, you know. It's somebody else's baby as well. Half that baby belongs to some man. What about him?

– What about him? He doesn't care.

– How do you know? Have you asked him? I bet if he knew he would. What about me, what if he's me? I would.

– It's irrelevant, she says.

As her belly grows large and oval as an enormous egg she looks more like a decadent waif than ever. With her thin arms and legs she seems a puzzled child, victim of the wand-waving of some ambiguous fairy. Good or bad only patience will tell. Gerry has merely to think of her, see her in his mind, for his bowels to yearn.

But he can't do anything. Not make her stop smoking her skinny cigarettes, or eat more, or count vitamins, or go to exercise classes, or learn to breathe. Cunningly–for he thinks they have a faint counter-culture air–he brings up home birth, midwives, Nursing Mothers. People say they're marvellous. So natural.

– Natural, pig's bum. Interfering busybodies.

He hasn't bought anything new for the flat or done any do-it-yourself for ages. The bachelor pad impetus seems to have left him. He looks around, and wonders where they could put a baby. There's only one bedroom. Best bet would be a bigger flat, or what about a house? Nothing wrong with a bit of investment in a mortgage, on his salary. And the kid'll need a garden to play in sooner or later.

He is obsessed with the child. His seed, his flesh. His bowels yearn for it.

– Listen, says Gerry, at eight months. Where are you going to put this baby? What are you going to dress it in? It's got all mod cons where it is, it's not going to be too impressed slumming it in an old beer carton wrapped in a teatowel or whatever you can find at the time. It'll probably turn up its toes and die.

– That's a point, she says, the nearest she's come to agreeing with him. I'll go down to Vinny's and see what they've got.

– No, says Gerry. He rushes off shopping with his bankcard, goes to posh baby shops and buys a basket and a bath, and nappies, and cute little suits, a teddy and a rattle, soap and powder, blankets and bunny rugs, and anything else the salesladies tell him he needs. All in blues, from very pale to navy. Perfect for either sex.

– Shit, you're turning the poor little bugger into a bourgeois monster before it's even born, says Sybil, but she doesn't seem to mind really.

He's always turning up at the Braddon house. You should move back in, says Don. Gerry keeps reminding Janet to make sure she tells him the moment anything happens.

– This is awfully nice of you, Gerry, she says, but for God's sake, Sybil's all right, she doesn't need it, you know. It's probably absolutely nothing to do with you. And Sybil doesn't care if it is.

He looks at her with gloomy miserable eyes. I reckon it's mine. I have to look after it. I can't trust my baby to Sybil.

More often when he turns up the house is empty. Not locked, that is part of the ethos. But empty, without strong Janet or fucking Mark or Don or skilful Sim, and certainly without Sybil; just the faint smells of garlic and coffee and that mustiness of human habiliment.

And then one day Sybil is there. Pottering about, melancholy, not angry. Her hair still fuzzy and dull, her face unpainted and meagre. She's wearing the thin-woven cotton shift, not camouflaging at all the bulk of the housed child.

She sits in one of the hippopotamus chairs, first pressing her hands into the small of her back, bowing her body, apparently offering her belly trembling to the world. Thus have women always stood, bearing the weight of their bellies. She sits down, tired; she looks worn, charming; still young, but worn.

Show me, he says, and she pulls up the Indian shift, and shows. The great curve of her belly is fawn-coloured, taut, faintly gleaming; more than ever like an enormous egg. He thinks of Sinbad and the Roc's egg, and the bird that fiercely hatching will carry him away. The dark fate, the dreadful years of exile, waiting to peck its way out.

And then the great shell wrinkles and he puts his hand there and then his mouth kissing it and feels the child's tiny fist punching or small foot kicking against his resting cheek, and he is so moved by this moving that he cannot contain his desire to wrap the fragile shell and its dear contents in his care and thought for ever. And Sybil leans back and lets his face rest against the great smooth egg of her belly and accepts apparently gratefully his care. The predatory bird flies away out of his mind.

– I would look after you so well, he says.

– Shall we screw? she asks.

He is shocked. His passion is tender, not erotic. But tenderness is sensuous and sensual, he finds he desires this closeness to both of them. To make love to Sybil, and the baby.

–But how can we? I'll squash you. Him.

–From behind. That's the best way of dealing with this bloody great bulge.

So he makes love sweetly from behind, folding his hands over her and feeling the baby move and imagining its pleasure like his own.

Afterwards he says, Marry me Sybil, you've got to marry me.

Sybil says no.

He asks her if he can be present at the birth. If you like, she says, amazing him. But when Janet rings up and he dashes off to the hospital he's too late. The baby is born.

A girl. Remarkably pretty, he thinks. A pointed chin and round shapely face, not dew-lapped like a matron or jowled like a politician. The nurse holds her up safe behind the window, and he loves her.

– I'm calling her Jade, says Sybil. He'd like a flowery romantic name, Belinda or Melissa or Rosamund, but knows there's no point in saying so.

He comes every day. Brings flowers, grapes, books. She laughs that he should be so boring. After a week she can go home. He arranges to take the afternoon off work and drive her. He's had a brainwave; shift all the baby's stuff to his flat and take Sybil there: dramatic gesture, *fait accompli*. But thinks better of it. Sybil's hobby is unravelling *faits accomplis*.

When he arrives at the hospital, Sybil isn't there. She has discharged herself this morning. He hurries round to Braddon. Nobody there either. The house unlocked. Sybil's things gone, and some of the baby's. He goes to the Union Bar. Nobody there from the house. He has some beers to fill in the time till people are likely to get back for tea. The beer is a last resort; he wants to act, but can't think how, and buying beer after beer is a sort of action, something to do while he works out the scope of really significant deeds. And has the advantage of making their necessity seem less immediate.

The prunus are red in the street outside the Braddon house, plum foliage painted in thick strokes over the bare twigs of winter. And then the wind comes and the leaves flash silver shards amid the bloody red and mock his stumbling passage. The trees are beautiful, fixed, and full of life and he poor beery lurcher mindlessly ambulant can never achieve a being so intense as they. They shiver with laughter and he stumbles and stops and pisses vengefully against a trunk and feels his self drain away at the foot of this powerful blood-red tree. His body sags against it, his face presses into the prickly bark, tears run out of his eyes. He is draining all away. He sags against the tree and weeps.

– Well, bugger me, says Janet, coming home in dirt-caked dungarees. Shit. Haven't a clue. She didn't tell me what she's up to. Could be anywhere.

The others say the same. Could be anywhere. Knowing Sybil. They sit around shaking their heads and drinking beer. After a while Mark says.

– Murwillumbah. She said something about going there once. Or was it Nimbin? Getting away from fucking civilisation and all that. Fucking Murwillumbah, that was it, I reckon.

– Could be, says Janet. Just the sort of thing she would do.

– Yeah, says Sim. Figures.

Murwillumbah. Or Nimbin. He empties another can of beer. It's not a lot. But it gives him somewhere to start looking for his baby.

SOMETIMES WHEN WE FUCK

Jacqueline Barrett

Sometimes
When we fuck
I grow extra parts.

The flop soft flop
Of your silky sack
Taps greetings on my arse
Until our transformation
To one creature makes it
My
Scrotum;
Just as your bony ribs
Grow my breasts,
And they are our breasts,
And our nipples are
Tongued stiff by the pleasures
Of all our several tongues.

You lose our fingers often
In the confusion,
Sweating through steamy marshlands,
Searching new handholds
In hairforests.
The moaning cries of animals out
In the dark of our borders
Send their warmth and odours in
Upon us, almost lost.
And we open all these overlapping
Petals, here,

Until I hear our voice
Start in my head, to
Escape from your mouth,
Calling
I love you I love you I
Love
You.

NOW THAT'S EROTIC

Diane Brown

I'm lying in the missionary position inside a caravan –1–2–3–4 birth! I twist my head back, look over my shoulder, up through the big window of the caravan. I can see bright green banana leaves blurring against blue sky. This is the Tropics. Get it while it's hot. She's putting off another college deadline. She'd rather be sailing to somewhere exotic like Vanuatu. And she says, 'I want to fuck you hard,' and I say, 'Go, baby, go!' And they call this place Fannie Bay.

Outside my bedroom window, walls pulsating pink, there's a tall clump of Bird of Paradise. I can see them from my bed as I work my clitoris. A woman's work is never done. Trying to remember to breathe, hold, breathe. When I climax on windy days I can watch the orange and scarlet flaming heads burn.

Erotica are the holes I've rubbed in my tee-shirt I wear at night to keep me warm. Just by turning over and over on my right side, left side, right, the friction of fabric against nipple has worn two perfect peep holes.

I

Remember dancing with the boys at school socials? Pimply perverts. They'd pull you real close and hold your waist as tight as a rubber ring round a lamb's tail. Their swelling cock against your ironed frock, crushing your corsage of sweet violets, maidenhair and forget-me-nots, until they had a hard on, red-faced, ease their grip, look away, grin at their mates . . .

II

I'm standing opposite a woman on the dance floor in a women's bar. The music is pounding. 'I am what I am. No more excuses.' I am mesmerised. We are thrashing about, slipping and sliding, up and down, round and round. Swimming together like eels. She is watching me. Watching me. Herbreastsarmsthighs. Swimming, swimming. She is grinning. I am. So wet. We are not even touching. I am going to come. We are not even touching.

The first time, a big space opening, opening. A sea eagle spreading her wings. And then the eagle took flight, soared and spiralled. Below, in the eye of the spiral, silver fish jumped again and again, in and out of the sea, a silver flickering tongue. Deeper, much deeper, soft sea anemones. Octopus touch tentacles rise to the surface in the eye of the spiral. Air and water meet fire. The eagle has landed.

KEEPING FIT

Dorothy Horsfield

It was three months or so before she became one of the regulars. There were, she reckoned, about two dozen.

For a start, a handful of elderly women came in the mornings about eight thirty. They were full of girlish good-humour, calling greetings to each other, floating about in the water, chatting. They wore baggy floral costumes with plastic cones in the front, their bodies bulging and barrel-tummied, skin like mottled old apples. Mostly they breast-stroked up and down for ten minutes or so, then sat in the spa at the side of the pool. Sometimes they took morning tea there, sipping it slowly in the bubbling water; or they lay back spreading arms along the tiled sides, luxuriating. They looked so strange, she thought, with their hair plastered to their scalps, their crumpled faces – like ugly, alien creatures – beyond vanity.

In the change-room she caught snippets of their conversations: 'Right there it was, the lump, big as a man's fist. You could've knocked me over with a feather.' You'd expect them to be like that, she thought, reduced to the drama of their diseases. She wished they'd do some proper exercise, wondering why they bothered to come at all, at their easygoing acceptance of bodies so bloated by decline and decay.

It doesn't really matter, she told herself, acknowledging that such thoughts were unkind, even spiteful. It was just that seeing them so often, she'd begun to feel a personal interest.

There was her friend, Ena, who must've been in her eighties. Shaky, arthritic, she was helped into the water by her gentleman friend. When she wasn't up to swimming, Ena walked the length of the pool.

'I been watching you,' Ena said. 'You keep at it.'

Pushing forty herself, she took this advice to heart.

'For Godsake,' John said, 'go somewhere else. You're becoming morbid.'

She was used to the place and she liked to watch the passing parade. Going there, she also accomplished something. It gave focus to days blurred by the care of three small children, by housework, dinners to be cooked. It wasn't that she resented such demands. She wanted keenly for those around her to feel well nurtured, to grow in love and strength. It was something else – the passing of time, the feeling that she would wake up to find her sense of herself had slipped away.

There were a few oddballs at the pool, with that remote, abstracted look, keeping themselves to themselves: the skinny woman in shower cap and underwear who must've thought she was in a bathhouse; the tiny foreign lady with the black moustache who sat in the children's pool soaking up the chlorine; and the tall man with the pot-belly who wallowed through the water, splashing and kicking, standing up every couple of metres to launch himself again. He couldn't swim for peanuts, but he kept going, oblivious, hogging a lane to himself. She'd often seen him hawk noisily into the water. Next time she meant to complain about it.

She went each day through the Canberra winter. The water had a tropical warmth. There were clumps of foliage everywhere, hanging ferns, massive monstera and philodendron that were replaced when the leaves curled and turned brown. The air was thick with chemical steam, lifting the paint off the ceiling. On one side a bank of windows looked out on the park. Once, backstroking her ten lengths, she glimpsed the frozen rain turn to floating snow. When she came out, the parking lot was white. It made her feel hardy, enduring.

When she didn't make it in the mornings because she was tired – had been up to the kids during the night – she went at lunchtime. It was a different crowd, muscled and lean, indistinguishable from each other in caps and goggles. They churned through the water at twice her speed – the sort who swam two kilometres during lunchbreak and jogged in the evenings.

'They're a bloody bore,' John said. 'And they'll be dead before they know it. Look at Jim Fixx.'

John was the paunch and slippers type, she thought, determined to slide comfortably into middle age. He had a lot of arguments against exercise.

'Jogging's a massive assault on the human skeleton.'

'It weakens the ligaments in the ankles, the knees, the pelvic joints.'

'It invites an early coronary.'

'Swimming's all right but not in chlorinated pools.'

'Daily exercise is unnatural. I get enough of it, walking up and down the stairs at work.'

She knew what he was getting at. Keeping fit had become a cultural obsession, a crusade, the Fountain of Youth, the New Puritanism. It went hand-in-hand with food fads – beetroot juice purgatives, homegrown bean sprouts and tofu custard. Take-aways and fat rump steaks were like snake venom.

It was narcissistic too. She looked at herself often, tucking in her bottom and pushing back her shoulders. The aim was to be sinewy, thin as a Masai warrior, with ridges of muscle outlined against the skin.

Never mind the broken veins in her legs, the dimples on the backs of the thighs, her puckered stomach.

'Those are the insignia of age,' John shrugged, 'like Brownie badges.'

She wasn't so sure. In the harsh fluorescent light above the change-room mirror she could see the mesh of lines round her eyes, the thickening of the flesh on her jawbone. Three feet away, there was the image of the younger woman, the Ghost of Beauty Past. Not so the close-up. Growing old was an ambush – turn around and it zapped you.

At twenty she'd strutted her stuff in slinky mini-dresses, halter tops and skin-tight jeans, breathing in deeply to zip them up. She'd been lovely with slanting sensual eyes and long glossy hair. At parties or down the pub she juggled lovers, holding out for something special. The trouble was knowing if you'd found it; if what you had now – marriage, kids, the whole domestic ballgame – was that it? enough? everything she could've hoped for?

Two decades on, options had narrowed. She'd learnt to bow before contingencies. She supposed she'd mellowed. There was no point, she thought, in those jabs of bitter restlessness.

Sometimes after her swim she sat in the change-room with Ena, listening to the old woman's tales of love affairs, fancy young men, marriage. She was a great talker.

'I loved my bit of fun,' Ena boasted. 'Course the old fella never found out. He was a terror – would've beaten me black and blue.'

Ena dressed herself slowly while she talked, lifting heavy arms into her blouse, bending painfully to smooth her stockings up the legs. Her swollen fingers scrabbled with her shoelaces. She painted herself as a bit of a character, goodnatured and bawdy. It was an old woman's way of defying illness, of giving herself courage.

I wouldn't be like that, she thought; I'd be the mean old biddy in the wheelchair swatting people with my walking stick.

Listening to Ena, she saw that old age came too quickly, was always half-unexpected. She thought of herself, 'a tattered coat upon a stick', with only a grab-bag of memories to cling to. She wanted to know how you came to terms with it all, with proper grace and dignity.

At Christmas, down the coast, nursing the baby under the trees while the older kids played in the sand, she'd watched a woman on a surf-ski. She was superb, like a gymnast, balancing, manoeuvring, flipping in and out of the breaking waves. She was burnt dark brown and wore a skimpy bikini. Her yellow hair was pulled up in a ponytail.

Later, on the beach, she'd seen that the woman was quite old, perhaps in her sixties. Even close up, she kept that illusion of youthfulness; as if, for her, growing old were simply the weathering of what was, at heart, untouchable.

Some of the men at the pool were lovely. But the Adonis was really something. He was a fine swimmer with powerful shoulders and a tiny bottom. He wore a sort of G-string. His hair was a blond curly mess.

'He's beautiful,' she said to John, 'like a painting.'

'Fancy him, eh? Shocking, an old lady like you!'

She was irritated by that. She told herself she never thought much about having an affair, not seriously. She was there strictly for the exercise. Besides, when you're single you give out subliminal messages, the body language of seduction. She was out of practice.

There were young girls at the pool, high-breasted and sexy. They swam in little stretchy costumes cut high across the buttocks and low at the top. They spent ages getting dressed, blow-drying their hair, teasing it stiff with gel, applying mascara and scarlet lipgloss, turning this way and that. They were self-absorbed, intent on a precise transformation: the rag-bag look – underplaying their sensuality with sloppy clothing, Op shop style. Their faces were overdramatic like whores, but innocent too under a halo of crinkly hair; or punk with pasty make-up and purple eyeshadow, the hair short and severe like Edwardian dykes. They were so confident, sure of provoking envy and admiration.

As she wriggled out of her navy Speedo and stood naked, her skin with its grey, doughy pallor of winter, they would glance at her dismissively.

I'm right out of it, she thought, invisible, beyond comparisons.

'That's the trouble with getting old,' Ena'd said. 'No one wants to touch you anymore. Packaging's gone to pot.'

When the Adonis began to greet her, flashing a big smile, she conceded to herself she was flattered.

'You don't have to worry, luv.' Ena winked. 'You're doin' all right.'

Sometimes he swam in her lane, pausing after a couple of lengths to wait for her.

'How y'doing?'

'Fine.'

'Listen,' he said, 'keep your knees straight when you kick.' He held onto the side and demonstrated. 'With your heels just tipping the top of the water.'

He was so earnest. 'You'll go faster.'

She wondered what he was really like, what to make of it. Mostly she thought the whole thing was ridiculous, her Mrs Robinson complex – the woman of experience and the chancy young man. Still, she wove a few small daydreams about him; that he was subtle and sensitive, shy like her behind his smiles; and intuitive, a real lover.

He waited for her in the foyer. 'You don't have to rush off. Come'n have a cup of coffee.'

He gripped her shoulder, steering her out the door across the road to the milkbar with tables and chairs down the side. A cappuccino for her; he had a double chocolate thickshake, sucking up the foam at the bottom like a kid.

'Do a lot of swimming?'

She nodded.

'Yeah, I'm on a tight programme,' he said. 'Mornings I do an hour, usually get it up to three and a half kilometres. Try to put a lotta, y'know, variation into it. Five hundred butterfly, bit of backstroke. Know what I mean? I'm a freestyle man. That's me strong one. Like to get on the weights – not over there; equipment's not, y'know . . . up-to-date. Go out to Phillip six nights a week.'

He couldn't sit still. He kept massaging his arms and rotating his shoulders to loosen the muscles. Maybe I should crack my knuckles, she thought, challenge him to an arm wrestle.

'You ever get in the spa?' he said. 'Don't go for it, myself. All those bodies, in and out, full of germs.'

He looked straight at her. 'Listen, you ever get lonely? Like some company now and again? Know what I mean?'

She couldn't help smiling; so much for love poetry in the moonlight. She could've taken offence at the suggestion in his words that his body was something special – for which she might be grateful.

She stood up, leant across and patted his cheek. 'I'm off. Have to pick up the baby.'

Next morning she bought some goggles to protect her eyes from the chlorine. They made her look like an insect. But she loved the sensation of swimming with her head under water, eyes open, watching the strokes of her arms and feeling her body twist and kick rhythmically. She was in a world apart.

'How's the work of art?' John asked, as they lay quietly after making love.

'What?'

'Your secret passion?'

She flicked off the bedside light and snuggled up to him in the darkness. 'Honey, he's just a pretty face.'

Sex in the Modern State

Joanne Finkelstein

The New York Review of Books Personal Column

SWM professional with eclectic tastes from opera to roller skating. Wants SWF interested in everlasting entertainment.

Rubens female, lively, humanistic enjoys conversation, culture, the beach. Seeks emotionally well-proportioned male counterpart. Photograph requested.

Fitness fiend loves hanggliding, bicycling, nature. Self-aware, auto-didact, strictly het. Wants slender other who can interface business and leisure.

We arrange our personal tastes as if they were stock in a bourse. We advertise, sell, expect a guarantee of quality, pay only to possess. After all, in a fast world, what is before you this moment is all that counts and that makes the body the only fact. We are too sophisticated to believe in making history and the future; there is no question of participating in the body politic, of paddling the race further through the evolutionary mists towards civilisation. It is now that matters, the entertainment, the sense of being consumed and consuming; the body is the ballast.

The only body available is our own. Its universal musculature and skeleton is our stock. We can trade it for sociality by stretching its proportions and disguising its peculiarities. Happily, it is a common language, so that when we are on the beach, in the bar, at the gym, across the table, we can with the most cursory of glances assess the body before us for its yin/yang, and gauge immediately the future together. The body summarises our desires; it encodes, processes and connects us; it is a charm, plaything, and gift.

THE DICK CAVETT SHOW/APOSTROPHES

If I met —— —— my life would stop. I would stand before him/her
my arms partially lifted, shaping me into the arrow-like wedge of an ancient
direction, and I would utterly surrender. In his/her dark magnificent frame
I would realise the pains of old complaints, of love misunderstood, conver-
sations unended, morality undone, strength unrewarded. S/he would wrap
protective arms about me, whisper knowingly, domesticate the pain, gently
perform a miniature, frontal lobotomy.
  My life and love, love and life finally fused.

Permission to be sexual has been granted to a huge population from
the prepubescent to the over seventies, to the tubercular, the car-
diac, the psychologically unstable, the transsexual, unmarried, and
physically disabled. Sexuality is the lingua franca through which
we collectively speak. Irrespective of our income, gender, and
privileges, we are similarly buffeted by its ebb and flow. It is both
democratising and prosaic. Sex is the thread unifying, binding, self-
imprisoning the species. There is not a setting or circumstance or
ceremony from which sex has been dismissed. We take its nagging
presence in the absurd and unexpected moments of the everyday as
a welcome sign of our vitality and as a proof that we are civilised.
There is sperm, mucus and sweat in the library, cinema, boardroom,
surgery, confessional, street, elevator, kitchen, car, lobby, toilet,
corridor, bus, mall, swimming pool, in the classroom, between
classes, behind the podium, in front of the windows, on top of the
stairs, on the television. We do not know where it should and
should not be found. If it is purely biological, then it is spontaneous
and necessary to our health and it must be welcomed into the library
and public street. But, if it were otherwise, then we would have to
explain its ubiquity, and that might suggest our vacuity.

Without the rush of blood, without the desire for oceanic sen-
sations, without sex, we are disquietened. The sexual gesture is the
point by which we are defined and organised. It is proof and demonstration of that urgency which portends our humanity. Consider
the alternative: the non-genital, the disinterested, the aged, ill and
foresworn, they are miscellany, odd trifles. It is by the acceptance
of sexuality in all aspects of our life that we think we have a right
to endure.

But what is being said when demonstrations of sexuality are the
hallmark of civility? when a rock singer collapses on stage in front

of thousands of people, with a microphone still clutched between the thighs, the head sagging, gagging over it? when the lunatic fringe in the radioactive horror show lament the future of children made into mutants who will never know the ecstasy of having a 'cue in the rack'? when bodies flying in response to a sense fatiguing disco throb, hips spread like inviting hands, trick one another into intimacy? when the cinema offers unearthly figures, freaks and the possessed who sensuously wrap themselves about a languishing body to feast upon the detritus while an enthralled and thirsty audience sucks in the dark? when a woman is tattered, slaughtered by the pornography industry so that the entrepreneur, thug, poet, missionary and schoolteacher can feel strenuously enough to confirm their own abilities? when houses, bathroom towels, cars and crockery are presented not as utensils of the everyday but as aphrodisiacs and portals to the human essence?

Memoirs

I have lost interest in sex. It is like eating Indian or Greek food; I have the aesthetic response but not the bodily. Perhaps it is too much sex over the years, or too little good sex, or too much of other people's sex that has doused my interest. I find myself satiated without having tried it all. It is as if I had secretly gorged myself while in a somnambulistic state or been force-fed by a hungry voyeur. I am no longer moved by penile shaped cars or sofas like women's breasts. I now skim over every mound, cup, curve or rod that is subliminally hidden in my food and clothes.

Without an interest in sex, I began to worry about my mental health, so I took a lover much older thinking that age and experience would bring a new world of sensuality and pleasure. But the urgency of time and the fear of incapacitation made sex a gasping for life. Then, I took a lover much younger, thinking that I could review the ancient process of acquiring sexual tastes, but there were only soft kisses, endless strokes and pats that put me to sleep before waking me up.

I have lost interest in sex.

Throughout history there has been a fascination with the perverse body, with the bizarre and exotic. The popular forms of entertainment in the Victorian age were the circus, quacks of various kinds, hypnotists and the strange phenomena found in freak shows, who revealed the other side of humanity. It was the age, too, when studies of the human became formally incorporated into the academy, in the new disciplines of anthropology and psychology. The freak was a supernumerary yet the offspring of conventional sexual unions – the dwarf, hermaphrodite, bearded woman, Siamese twins, giant, elephant man and dog face were challenges to the legitimacy of the sexual act. They were its unanticipated results and forebodements of the terror of sexuality, the nightmare into which desire could dissolve. Lombroso, Krafft-Ebing, Havelock Ellis and Freud welded sex to character and character to civilisation with the good intention of improving us. Their studies of frotteurism, onanism, morbidity, lasciviousness, voyeurism and bestiality were for our benefit.

In the iron cage of the modern, the century of rationalism, order, bureaucracy and the state, the struggle to feel is equal to the power to repress. Sex has become an exaggerated behaviour that attempts to lift the pall from our senses and engender feeling where there can rightfully be none. The extent to which we are affected by extreme forms of sexuality – by pornography, romanticism, exotica – is a measure of how little we understand sex. In pornographic images, we find abhorrence and fascination. As we watch the bizarre, cruel, weird and surprising, we are both repelled and sexually alerted; under the social training there is a cannibalistic twitch. The bizarre succeeds in penetrating the pall; the irony is that in the extremes we begin to see normalcy.

DEAR DIARY

12 February 19–
I changed your life, you said, gave you courage, made your insides move, become voracious. I groomed your anger into a fine political tool, stood you up and pointed to the exit – at least, that is what you said. It was love, you said, that opened you, freed you to think and establish claims on life. It was passion and desire that exalted you, made you strong enough to smile, be nonchalant and ignore the daily squabbles with ——.

But, you still live with ——, go to the office each day, shop at the supermarket, measure a movie by the number of times you laugh, keep a cat.

So I say, it was sex, the mindless gyrations, that caught you. It was the reflexes, the nerve-endings, muscle spasms and not the sensibilities which moved.

Desire speaks of an absence. We calculate rather than talk, and if we imperceptively rearrange our limbs, if we harness the efforts of our partner without his/her knowledge or permission, if the tangle of limbs can become a choreography, then the immediate urge can be answered. The lover is a tool and the interior world remains undisturbed.

Our sexual practices shape the appetite. Now, we can dine in public, tease, touch, insist and seduce the other, with a stranger seated at our elbow, doing the same to his/her companion. The public is our private. We can speak to one another from street telephones, about family, quiet moments and nights together, as if there was no commerce buffeting us. We readily sleep and bathe in hotel rooms, use cafés for intimate meetings, excite ourselves in the dark auditorium of the public cinema. We go home to oblivion and step out to live. There has been a reversal of inner and outer and the happy consequence is that by seeking our hungers in the marketplace we think we have obliterated the possibilities of an unknown, terrifying interior.

Sexuality is no longer personal; the meaning of sex has been codified, externalised, placed within a canon, made traditional and imperious. The meaning of sex has been replaced by the imperative to be sexual. In the modern state, sex has been divided so that one version can be sold to the other. Industries have proliferated in the division, and then urge, even menace, us into reuniting in the sexual act, the human credential. The general categories of male and female are more than taxonomic; they are a doctrine of domestic order.

Sex in the modern state is a tortuous interplay of individuals moulded by anti-human desires such as ownership, conquest, control, self-aggrandisement. The proffered sex organs replace conversation and the struggle to make sense. The sexual gesture has been stripped of nuance and thought. Now it is a skill and technique which we advertise with our subscription to the *New York Review of Books*, a season ticket to the opera, a borzoi hound, leather clothes and a collection of Kundera. Now it is an emblem. The sexual gesture records a dreadful equation between ourselves and the social order.

EDGES

Jane Meredith

so we have come to the precipice.
and if you breathe i will fall off
into nothing.

there is a certainty that you will come. at whatever time. and that i will fall. (leave my writing and the night.) if that certainty did not exist . . . there would be no solid ground on which to stand. from which to write. even of you. and the clock ticks, anyway.

the possibility that this is the last time i will wait for you, that this is the last time you will come to me is so real it has become tangible. it is at least as real as any memory i have of you of us, even

head back against the pillow throat naked gasp of breath through slight body
hands against me holding eyes flickered closed lashes taut lithe delicate desire
snaking wrapt gently cradling against within your face above mine holding
to kiss hands stroked along around breasts against my body strength in
control/release watching you/me

i have made that up. it never happened, or – so long ago that it can have no bearing on tonight. its reality has faded, now my imagining of tonight is surer, truer than memory's construction, less gentle than fantasy can be.

when you come in something irrevocable will have happened to your face and i will never see you the same way again.
    and you will tell me quietly, with ultimate control standing beside the fire maybe leaning on the mantlepiece head slightly

tilted as if to catch some half-heard indefinable air that it is over. and in moderated tones explain. not enough; there can never be enough explanation to suffer this, to create reason for it. it means nothing, only end.

and yet i do remember a time, a night, not unlike this night, this time that is related to that time by the strength of you, the night, the waiting of me when the world was perfect. when it never could have been that i would look at you to see that something irrevocable has happened in your face and i will never see you the same way again. when there could never be enough nights to wait for you, knowing that you will come, when i could not have believed that there would ever be an end to them and now there is only one and there will be no solid ground on which to stand, only end.

patrolling a corner of my mind, as yet contained, is the sick horror/fear of this reality. i want not to be this person, not to be here, not to know this, be trapped here in the circle of this realisation (terror) reality (despair) existence (insanity) inevitability inescapable finality/death means the end of life and in that second (the end) all that counts is only life (and light, not dark) even as it darkens.

i remember crying childlike in despair at your anger, inexplicable fear – perhaps then i glimpsed this – that this would change you, would finally show what i always knew inside me (inadequacy) and yet i do remember that you came to me and held to you in comfort against the dark fear fierce tears tearing again apart the sanity or strength that holds together (mostly) composing my self. i do remember that, and the enormity of feeling echoed now is less gentle than fantasy can be and so real it has become knowledge, it has created now its own reason to exist; the end.

it's when i stop writing, lift my mind from the white page and the shapes the words make against it that the descent of fear consumes all thought; then there has to be existence through a time where there is no longer any hope when a desperate spiral/need to close my eyes curl down small caught into a corner slow breathing stop thinking not being drowning in self-inspired desperation.

and yet the clock still ticks and i know you will come. to me and for the last time maybe, but you will come to me and shall i walk towards you at the door or stand back, will i turn away my head as you speak or watch your eyes in their betrayal will i touch your hand again will i ever kiss or feel your lips against mine lost seconds

that i cannot say existed if they will never be again.
there is devastation in the thought that i will never wake again to soft kisses across the back of my neck and this is more real than any memory i have of you.

the only reality to my mind is the certainty that you will come, at whatever time and that the clock still ticks which means that time is still passing which means that every word moves me closer to the end. these are the certainties that keep me moving through this time and that, with me, are spiralling towards the time that you will get here and it will end and time will no longer count or be counted because you will be here and it will be the end. and all this is only to be broken by you, you who are the reason for the writing, for moving through this time at all in any way, you who are the certainty which is what you bring, the end.

and i wonder idly, straying from the thought and page what peculiarities, what unpredictable details will occur in this occasion will you be wearing will your hair how will you in what ways where will we will your hands be will you look at me will i speak will anything between us be there or will you only how will i react how will i cope and all of these details catch the eye because as yet they are beyond reality, they are yet to be and i can speculate, imagine. how would it be if you ignored me and i cried, how might it feel if you were passionate and i argued, would it seem more logical if we were both polite and all this whirl of possibilities can exist because they have a gravity to what will happen, to why you have come and why i am here now, waiting for you.

it is so simple that i have had a dream that i was happy and it was a dream. even before you wake you realise the difference between the dream and being awake and that difference and knowing that you are between those two possibilities and one is a dream and one is being awake is the solid ground even if neither of those two things is. and only the clock ticking brings reality closer.

i am scared like i was scared when i was four of the nameless horror dark of nothing being there no one ever and i will have to fight to even live it is waking up and the nightmare is real it is waking up to the nightmare it is waking up and the dark is all that is left there is no comfort — why hope? this is the only time and place this is where i am this is the only hope and solid ground has caved beneath my feet.

and you are here. and i open the door to you (step forward, and yes you are wearing) and you kiss me on the cheek as you pass in to stand against the fireplace (and yes you look at me) and we have come to the precipice and speak of common things and you have come and nothing else has ever happened and not this time. and the clock ticks.

SEVEN FOR A SECRET NEVER TO BE TOLD

Joan Birchall

Why won't you see me, Sabina? After all these phone calls, your avoidance of places where I may be. I am – astonishing as it seems – realising I am not going to see you again.

My return has been so sweet. Honeyed words, thick with care. The others have not forgotten me in all these years, so how could you? Don't you want to see my face and hear my traveller's tales?

I can hear you whispering, sibilant, soft as cream. My senses slow, become dreamlike. I am a little drunk. I remember how pleasant it was . . .

There is something else I should remember, some key to your reluctance. I have forgotten. There was some intoxication all that time ago.

We two, Sabina, white bloused, black-stockinged, gliding along corridors, arms entwined. Sitting together on seats, watching.

Is your hair still a black polished cap, Sabina? Does it shine in the sun the way I recall when we watched the birds fly past and counted, one for sorrow, two for joy, three for a letter, four for a boy. Five for silver, six for gold, seven for a secret, never to be told.

The secrets between you and me were many. The whispering blows through my mind, rustling the memories.

I can hear your piano-playing. Languidly the notes drift out through the open window on to the lawn, to dance like motes in the summer inertia. The sensuous afternoons seem so long.

Walking in the winter, we come upon a swollen stream. It falls heavily, bucking, rampant, foaming, roaring over the rock ledge. I see its frenzied madness reflected in your face glistening in the chill air.

Fog rolls through my mind. I can see you walking beside me in a cobblestoned alley. The fog eddies all about us. You whisper . . . Strange lewd knowledge. I listen spellbound, fascinated. Tell me more. Your head touches mine as you lean close to whisper and we walk into the white mist.

I watch the flames from the fire dancing in the grate. I can see pictures there. Strange red flaring demons quickly touch, turn and flee up the chimney. Some stay, laughing in a crazy cackle, spitting and hissing in derision. And in that scarlet haze, you pass the book to me, thick, heavy, red-bound and I handle it carefully like dynamite. It is burning my fingers, but you force me to keep hold, your fingers meanwhile flicking open the thin yellow pages to show pictures. Ugly pictures, strange, ancient, foreign. Naked turbanned men, fat-thighed black-haired women. I look away from the contorted figures, the obscene couplings, the vacant expressions. I look into the fire and the demons laugh again and again.

In the autumn we sit together on the moors among the purple heather and we read aloud, you taking Heathcliff to my Cathy. I am suddenly uneasy, when your dark eyes smoulder just as his did, but the afternoon is all-embracing, sufficient and warm.

Ah, now the play's the thing. Rehearsing, your hero to my heroine. With your short hair and your knowing eyes, you are more like a real man than those louts in the boys' school.

'Jolly good, Sabina!' Miss Emery calls as you finish your big scene.

The ballroom lessons, you leading. We must look at our feet in the long mirrors on the walls. You are growing so tall and straight. Your body is hard. There is something wrong with me. I'm getting softer.

I can feel the rain gentle on my face as we come out of the low hut deep in the woods. The damp ferns surround us. There are giggling girls, faces pressed against the window panes, looking out into the wet green world. It rains one day after another. We tire. We are bored. We read, lolling on our bunks. The giggling turns to whining, complaining.

'Do we have to stay the whole week? Camping!' Miss Emery smiles brightly, heartily. We must all put on our Wellington boots and raincoats and come for a ramble in the rain.

'It is so very pleasant in the summer rain,' she says, 'Listen to the birds.'

Your face is dark, sullen. You pull me back as I move out into the sweet freshness.

'Come on, Sabina.' I laugh, but you don't smile back.

You look at me, but never smile all through our walk and when we get back and cook our sausages on the verandah at the back of the hut, you are still not smiling. I drape my arm about your shoulders, but you are unyielding.

Our bunks are side by side, and we lie there at night with the rain falling gently, slowly touching the roof and the branches of the trees brushing, swishing softly, rhythmically.

I am in that weakened state just before sleep, when I feel you moving into my bed, your arms enfolding me, your hands gently stroking my skin. It is as soporific as the rain. My inner thigh is like satin in your hands.

Somewhere high within my secret places a serpent flicks and I leap out of bed before it strikes.

I feel foolish, as, without a word, you move back into your own bunk.

'Sabina.' I whisper, but you lie like something dead.

They tell me you went on to become a great educator. In earnest voices they tell me how privileged are the girls you teach.

And deep within my mind, I can see the rain dripping from the leaves on to the ground in the wet woods.

I would have liked to see you, Sabina. Do you remember the birds? How we watched them soar and counted as they swept across the sky.

I can remember the secret now, but I had forgotten Sabina, I had forgotten.

Two Photographs

Susan Hawthorne

Two photographs, taken five years apart, lie on the table in front of her. One taken by a man, a stranger. One taken by a woman, a lover.

I remember the first time I went there. A dark grey terrace house in West Melbourne. It was early evening, winter. I knocked on the door. A young bearded man answered.

'I'm Virginia Moore.'

'Come in.'

We went up some ricketty wooden stairs to the studio – a bare room with black curtains covering one wall and a series of photographer's lights beaming at an imaginary point.

'Take your clothes off,' he said matter of factly, as he went about the business of focusing his camera and adjusting the lights.

I undressed tentatively in the corner.

He looked me up and down approvingly.

'Stand there,' he said pointing to a spot in front of the black curtains.

'Fi-ine.' The shutter clicked.

'Look towards the corner. No, don't smile.'

What am I doing here? I thought.

'Now kneel. That's right. Stretch your hand forward. Now look up. Fi-ine.'

I'm here for the money, I reminded myself.

'Use your hand to sweep the hair from your face. Goo-ood.'

I cut off from the sense of exposure.

'Turn your head to the right. O-kay.'

I moved to his commands.

I began to sweat under the hot lights. I looked into them and was momentarily blinded. They were like interrogation lights.

'Okay, that'll do, you can get dressed now.'

I assumed I'd passed the test. 'When do I start?' I asked.

'Let's see, it'll take a day or so to print these. How about next Wednesday afternoon. Come at two o'clock. These will be your folio pictures.'

'Uh huh,' I murmured.

'Angie will be here on Wednesday to let you in, and she'll fill you in on what to do. Okay?'

'Yeah, I guess so.'

She looks at the first photograph. It is dark. Her body is the only light thing. Her expression is typical. There's a certain vulnerability in the way the lips part. She has seen the expression before in men's magazines. She must have remembered it and put it on for the occasion. Her hair tantalisingly covers part of her breast. She does not look at the camera.

I went back the following Wednesday. Angie was there.

'The photos of you are good,' she said.

'Oh, are they? Show me.'

Angie picked up the book that lay on the desk. She flipped quickly past the pages that had her sprawled nakedly across them. 'Here,' she said.

I looked at myself. I barely recognised the face that looked across the photograph towards some far away point of blankness. My breasts seemed larger than usual.

'They're good,' encouraged Angie. 'You'll have plenty of customers.'

'Do you think so, really?'

'Yeah, sure. Don't worry about it. The guys come in with their instamatic cameras. They flick through the book here and pick out the one they like. Then they have half an hour, or an hour to take their photos. There are some things they're not allowed to do though. They're not allowed to touch you, at all. If they do they forfeit their money and their remaining time. Okay?'

'Yeah. But what if they do?'

'Give us a yell. Or just get up and walk out. Or remind them that they're not allowed to. They'll stop, mostly. They're walking a fine line legally. Anyway, most of them know the routine – they're nearly all regulars.'

I had one session that day. A young man with an instamatic, just as Angie had said. It was easier than the first night. He didn't seem to mind what I did. I just moved around slowly. It was like doing a slow exercise routine.

I went home reassured and twenty dollars richer. I told no one. Twice a week, on Wednesday and Friday afternoons, I dressed up and went out and earned what I could. I stopped worrying about it soon enough. The money made it worth it. If anyone asked where I'd been, I said I'd been to the city. I frequently came home with new things, so no one doubted me.

An older man came in one day. Angie introduced me as the 'new girl'. He flicked through my folio and asked to photograph me. I went upstairs with him. He was friendly, in a paternal way.

'You like doing this?' he asked.

'It's okay . . . for a crust.'

'Bend forward and look up at the same time.'

I was on hands and knees, like an animal. My hair almost covered my face. I lifted my hand to brush it back.

'Don't move. That's lovely. Stay there. Let's have another.'

I sat back on my heels and looked at him briefly. The skin on his face was flabby and loose. There was nothing attractive about him.

'These'll be lovely,' he said, pleased with himself. 'Would you like a copy?'

'No, it's all right.'

'I'll bring you one anyway. Will you be here on Friday?'

'Yeah, Friday's my other day.'

'Okay, I'll see you then. Perhaps we could have a drink.'

'Perhaps,' I said noncommitally.

I did go in, and Angie and I went to the pub with him. He gave me the photograph. It was still wet. I don't remember his name.

Two photographs.
One taken by a man, a stranger.
One taken by a woman, a lover.

She looks at the second photograph. It is soft greys, merging into areas of darkness. It shows just a breast with an erect nipple. She remembers the day it was taken. It was taken with her new camera, which she'd bought duty free on her return from Britain.

I was lying on my bed in the house in North Fitzroy, pleased to be home, to be back with Denni. We were making the most of these first few days, spending our days and nights in bed. Occasionally making a journey into the outside world, to shop or pursue some other hedonistic activity. We went to the gardens, fed the black swans and drank coffee.

Denni sat opposite me, camera in hand. 'How do you focus it?' she asked.

'Just turn the lens bit round until you get a straight line across the circle in the middle.'

'Oh yes, I see what you mean.'

'What're you taking?'

'Just that lovely nipple of yours,' she said. 'Now, smile.'

'Why should I smile if you're only taking the nipple?'

'It makes a difference to the nipple.'

Two photographs.
One taken by a man, a stranger.
One taken by a woman, a lover.

GARDENIA

Donna McSkimming

father, something tugged at me today,
a cloud, nudging in the dark
uncomfortable memory over-warm on my skin,
in a place I rarely go
in a climate where they should not grow
I found today,
Gardenia.

& some languor touched me,
treacherous currents belly filling
as I ached to arc my back & moan
& watch indolence spill – a tropical deluge,
pouring ivory & gold from my mouth,
& that scent which must be drunk in great gulps
all senses stretched, the moment absolute
as taking poison or hallucinogens:
each exhalation a withdrawal & craving
that torpor begin its carbuncle unction
through my limbs.

how we succumb, father.
hearing your voice dictate,
the flowers must not be handled
– bruising spoils the show
& your severe pruning each season
down to stick.
& your disgust if Gardenia
dared appear deep in the bush
hidden from your calculating

to best effect.

& your beating, father
after I'd picked every one
in the rain at night
the flower's nimbus the only evocation of light.
& strew my bed in some adolescent passion
– perhaps for you, father.
& rolled & rubbed Gardenia
over lips & thigh & breast
smothered & drank deeply
as I do now unrepentant,
father.

I watch Gardenia
lustrous points in the dark
know the edges already begin to singe
curling tight as paper to disappear
in puffs like incense.
I know this flower grew in acid soil
revelled at noon's intoxication,
& am reminded father
of a day star blazing at full meridian
or buds exploding in my lover's eyes
or a fragrance like Gardenia petals
on her eyelids, each morning,
as I kiss them,
father.

The Man with the Magic Phallus

Leone Sperling

My husband and I have what is called an 'open marriage'. We're a modern, sophisticated couple. We're sure that it's possible to have a stable marriage and a little extra-marital fun without hurting anyone. The only rule we have is that our affairs are to be subordinate to our marriage.

I already have a lover, but our relationship is floundering. There's a new man I fancy. I met him quite by chance. I've agreed to go out to dinner with him, and my husband approves. He's going to mind the children while I go out and enjoy myself. That's only fair. After all, I babysit while he's out with his mistress.

I meet this new man and we go to a Chinese restaurant for dinner. He is, in many ways, every woman's dream. He is totally charming, disarming, self-confident. There is a twinkle in his eye and an assurance in his bearing that says he can have any woman he wants. I tell him that I have a husband and a lover. He says that doesn't bother him at all. He is in no hurry. He has infinite patience and time. He does not rush me, push me or make any sexual advances. He sits back, quite sure that I will come to him, waiting for me to make the first move. During dinner he tells me delightful and humorous stories of his early life in Hungary. He tells me of war experiences, smuggling, screwing in telephone booths. I feel that here is a man who has really lived a full and adventurous life. I've never been so genuinely delighted in a man's company. My somewhat gloomy husband and my despairing lover shrink beside this handsome man who makes me laugh and laugh.

He still makes no move. He goes on being totally, effortlessly charming. I am very easily won. As we leave the restaurant and go to cross the road, it is I who take his hand. He responds with a pressure of warmth, but still takes no advantage of me. We sit in his car. Now it's his turn to move. He kisses me and I am surprised by the warmth and passion of his kiss. I can sense that he is a good lover, and I tell him so. He, evidently, feels the same about me. But there's no hurry. We arrange a meeting during the day in a week's time.

I go home and my husband's awake, waiting for me, wanting to know what I've done. What was he like? Did I go to bed with him? I don't want to talk about it. I want to be left alone. He makes me tell him all about the evening. I have to go over every detail – the dinner, the kissing in the car, the plans for a further meeting. 'You're going to go to bed with him, aren't you!' he says, his own excitement mounting. 'I know you are.'

'I'm not sure,' I reply, wanting to keep something to myself.

'Tell me again how he kissed you,' he demands, starting to make love to me. What he's asking me to do makes me shudder. He doesn't worry about foreplay but starts to thrust himself into me. 'Talk about it!' he says. 'Tell me what you feel when he kisses you.' I long to remain silent but I can't refuse him and I let the words he wants to hear tumble out of me. With a final, hammering charge he comes inside me, and then it's over and I'm glad it's over, and he lets me go, and I am, for the briefest moment, free.

The week seems long to me. I want this new man, and it feels good to be starting a new sexual adventure. When I get to his place and into his bed, I can see at once that I'm in the hands of an expert. He is cool, careful, perfect. He brings me to powerful orgasm with calm precision. Then he comes and, at that point, I am confronted with what I consider to be the eighth wonder of the world – his penis stays erect, and it is to remain that way for the next two hours.

Afterwards we talk. He tells me that I have a very rare sexual capacity and that, of the thousands of women he's made love to, only one other woman exhibited the strength of orgasm that I seem to be capable of. He proceeds to give a careful, scientific analysis of our lovemaking, trying to teach me to be aware of my vagina and its potential. He intrigues me. I've never met a sex expert before. He has, he admits, devoted his entire life, from the time he turned eighteen to his present forty-four years, to making love to women. I am, of course, delighted and flattered to find that I have such a capable cunt. He is the master, I the willing pupil. He lures me into a world where sex dominates, where orgasm is the prize, where all that is valued is the quality of the coming – an orgiastic banquet, a physical feast, where art of the performance rather than emotion is the measure of success. No breathtaking passionate hunger with him, but rather the slow, deliberate excitation, the building climb to passion, the holding back, the going forward, the artistic weaving towards the unbelievable come.

He is a shift worker and I work odd hours. We can fit in many daytime meetings. I go to his place five days a week. This excessive extra-marital indulgence contravenes the agreement I've made with my husband, but I don't care.

What is it that he is doing for me? It is not that he is making love to me but that he gives me free rein, allows me to examine and explore and extend my own sexuality. He is always in control, simply there – the ever-erect penis on which I work my own way, in my own time, to my own end. His orgasm is immaterial to him and to me. He is just the vehicle of my self-discovery. I teach myself to attain the mysterious multiple orgasm. I stop only when my legs ache or my back aches – my cunt could go on forever. I am Woman – powerful, unleashed.

I give myself totally to this awakened sexuality without regard to possible consequences. I am hooked, trapped, the willing victim of an insatiable lust. I am my cunt. Nothing else is.

My husband is furious. I have castrated him, reduced him to powerless frustration. He cannot compete. I throw in his face the fact that some other man is able to make me respond in this extraordinary way. It is intolerable to him to find that I have a sexuality that he could never unlock, a sexual expression that he will never witness. He feels bitter, rejected, jealous.

My other lover, whose relationship with me has been primarily intellectual, feels equally hurt. How can I, he wants to know, prefer sexual, animal gratification to what he has to offer? I thumb my nose at the two of them. I'd throw them both away for the man with the magic prick.

I become, for a while, a kind of sexual football. I am thrown among the three of them, being screwed into a stupor. Sometimes I go to bed with all three of them on the same day. I do it deliberately – just to see if I can climax with each of them. If my husband thinks I've been with either of the others, he wants me all the more. 'I don't care,' he says, 'I don't care who you screw as long as you save some for me.' And I don't care about anything at all any more. From morning till night my only thought is for the sexuality that has somehow taken over my being.

And what is he, this man of the magic phallus with whom I wallow and stuff and gorge my insatiable sexual gluttony? He is many things – professional gambler, smuggler, conman, thief. He entertains me constantly with stories of excitement and danger and I experience, through him, what it is to be an adventurer in an unstable and unpredictable world.

I am lying beside him. He is quiet at the moment. I am lying close to him, his arms around me. 'Have you ever killed anyone?' I ask, softly. I hear the 'Yes' from his heartbeat before I hear it from his lips.

Now I hear stories of a different kind – of murder and survival, of torture and imprisonment. He had been, he tells me, a smuggler with a difference. He had smuggled Jews out of communist Hungary and brought medicines and drugs back into the country. All this had been done for very high payment but within the boundaries of a strict, definitive moral code. He and his friend had been captured and imprisoned and his friend had been executed. He tells me now of torture, of having all his toe-nails pulled out and his teeth smashed. I understand now why his mouth is a glittering mass of gold fillings.

And then he tells me of revenge. Six guards, he says, inflicted torture upon him and, after his release from prison, he had sought out and killed five of them. The sixth came to Australia and he came here originally, he tells me, to catch and murder this man. I shiver beside him. Is he making this up? I don't think so. I sense his inner violence and I know that he is telling me the truth.

And all this explains something else about him. His heart is ice. He never feels. He is a machine. 'Don't ever fall in love with me,' he warns. 'I'm not capable of loving.' Of course, I do not heed his warning.

We have a big party at our house and I invite my new lover. He buys me an expensive, black, hand-embroidered, Rumanian dress. My husband is furious, but I don't care, and I flaunt my lover's generosity. He buys himself a black, silk shirt for the occasion, and he looks so suave and handsome.

At the party my lover ignores me. He dances all night with a friend of mine who does not know that he and I are lovers. I watch him flirt with her. I tell myself that my lover can't spend all evening with me. If he did, everyone would know that we are lovers and, as I'm still married, I should keep my affair secret. But I notice that my husband has no such sense of propriety, and he's deliberately staying with his mistress. I am mortified and would like the floor to open and swallow me up.

I know that my lover is having an affair with my friend. I sense it. I ask him outright and he denies it, but I know he's lying. I want to ask her but I can't. One day I see her driving along in her car. She has a dreamy, wanton, sexual look on her face. I know she's going to him. An hour later I drive past his flat and I can see that her car is parked outside.

I see him that night. I am full of venom, anguish, complaint, hostility, criticism. His face is impassive, the cold veneer I can never penetrate. No feelings there. Had he ever, he wanted to know, said he loved me? Had we ever agreed upon fidelity? He was my friend, my lover, always available when I needed him, his door always open, his cock always ready. What more did I expect?

'Love,' I wanted to cry, 'Love!'

POKING THE PEEVISH GUTTER

Stephanie Johnson

In the murkiest corner of the room, that is, the corner on the same side of the room as the door, the door that opens out into the corridor, the corridor with many doors leading off and away into many existences identical or at least similar to this one, something is moving. It is only just perceptible.

This room is perhaps a forest, or a ruined Roman temple rampant with crumbling and sometimes unnervingly tumbling columns. More like a forest though, as paper comes from wood, and that is what I am surrounded by – strata of newspapers, those catalogues of despair affordable by any man, woman or child, piled high one upon the other, reaching the ceiling in most instances and in others occupying only the status of the most uncertain sapling. And certainly this reconstituted copse has the density of the original. It cannot be seen through.

All I am sure of is that something is moving, the shadow of a shadow, shifting about near the cooker.

When Ferdie comes back I will ask him, once more, to open the curtains – if the curtains are still there, as it is difficult to tell even if the window is still there. Both the glass and my nearly forgotten geometric view are now wholly obscured. Perhaps Ferdie would switch on the light, first removing the pile of newspapers that last time filled the flatette with a terrible burning smell redolent of a bushfire kind of panic. But asking Ferdie anything is tricky: first to find the words, then to form them in a mouth the left half of which is paralysed, as is the left arm, eye, leg, foot, and worst of all hand; and secondly to endure Ferdie's taunting of me and my slack speech and slaver. To add to that I must find deep within myself a portion of the ever-decreasing fortitude that prevents a tear from slipping, new-born and innocent from my right eye, down my all but innocent and time-scored cheek. Either that or endure further mocking.

If Ferdie comes back. There is always a chance that he won't. He stayed away that night, the night after *she* came, the girl. Alerted, she said, by a neighbour, who wished to remain nameless, who rang them, the government department in the concrete and chrome tower devoted to making the lives – I should say, existences – of women like me, and perhaps a few unfortunate men, easier. Ferdie did not like the girl. The light from the corridor had shone behind her as she opened the door, turning her cloudy red hair to something holy, a halo, and the small gold crucifix around her neck picked up whatever light was left and tickled it about the room, playing on the columns. She was young, so very young, and her eyes widened at the sight of me. As she came in, Ferdie went out. She stood gingerly beside my yellow bed and asked me a number of questions, and understood, it was obvious, little of what I said in reply. I am good at detecting the misapprehension of another mind in the effort of grasping facts. During my life, and my life is all but over – you could scarcely call this existence a life – I was a schoolteacher, the English mistress at a girls' school, a school for the daughters of professional men and rich plumbers. Many times in the tuition of nobler instincts and passionate emotion such as these tanned and trivial girls had no notion of, I had seen this very same formation of the facial features. So very blank and not the tiniest degree of osmosis, although her pen on the clipboard did not stop moving for the briefest of seconds. Reluctantly she had lifted a sheet and examined my filthy nightgown and surrounds, and I confess I felt a glimmer of shame at the sight and smell. Mercifully her visit was brief, and she left with promises to return and improve matters with a more senior official, and I relaxed the tense responsive side of my frame to the pillows and waited, as I wait now, for Ferdie to come home. Only this time in the gloom I am not alone. Someone is shifting about, an unhappy spirit, the shadow of a shadow, the crumbling remains of someone who must need to be here, near me. I close my right eye, to ponder on who it might be.

Ferdie returns in a waft of alcoholic fume and grease from a near-completed meal of fish and chips. He is smiling, and places a soft chip between my lips, and follows it with a quick swig from a whisky bottle. The liquor affects me immediately and more potently these days, I imagine, because I am left with only half of my brain. Behind Ferdie's head as he tips the bottle once more down my throat, I watch the shadow from the other side of the room move close. Ferdie does not see it, so I will not point it out to him. Perhaps this presence is meant for me alone.

When Ferdie has fed me a fragment of fish and has reasoned in his foggy mind that that will be enough to keep me going, he pulls out yet another newspaper from under his arm and makes himself comfortable on the end of my bed, removing the pillow from under my head, opening the newspaper and reading. A few moments pass before he shows me the page-three girl, as he always does, with a sigh. I am surprised when he opens the top of my nightie and squeezes, none too gently, one of my breasts, the responsive right one.

'Nobody ever married you,' he says.

Ferdie has known this since the day he first arrived. That was before the stroke, and I had met him downstairs sitting on a biscuit box of his belongings, having just been evicted from his room for not paying the rent. He'd followed me up, me carrying a loaf of bread and a carton of milk and some smokes, asking himself in for a cup of tea and a sandwich, then helping himself to one after another of my cigarettes. It was a long time since I'd had a man in my room, the last one being my nephew reluctantly fulfilling a duty asked of him by my sister while he was here with the Royal Navy. And he hadn't stayed for long, and he hadn't drunk his tea. Sailors in port have better things to do than visit old aunties. Ferdie at least was appreciative of me.

'You talk nice,' he'd said.

Then I'd given him some money from the tin, and he'd gone and bought a bottle of port, which we'd drunk together. The next morning I had woken beside him, both of us still clothed and he with his shoes on, atop my bed. It was so nice to have company, and this, by the way, was what I had tried to tell the haloed girl when she came. The young have no idea of the loneliness one endures when one is old and ugly.

Ferdie never asked me to marry him, although you could say that for a while, before the stroke, which came a few months later, we lived as man and wife. We even had sexual intercourse on two different occasions, neither of which was satisfactory from my point of view, although Ferdie had wriggled and gasped and slept in that order. Those kinds of relations have always brought out the poetry in me – heaven knows why – it is an activity far removed from the tranquillity of the printed word. Ferdie, however, did not stir in me the kind of poetry I had loved as a girl being toppled by the boys from the Grammar School. In those days I was enamoured with Edna St Vincent Millay and murmured in waxy ears, 'What lips my lips have kissed, and when and why I have forgotten,' as an accompaniment to their adolescent pumpings. Ferdie heard me quote, as he slid to a heavy repose, from Mr Eliot, 'Here I am, an old man in a dry month, / Being read to by a boy, waiting for rain . . .'

At this moment, while the shadow rests behind a column out of Ferdie's sight, I should like to quote something further on from the same poem, something more appropriate: 'Think at last we have not reached a conclusion, when I stiffen in a rented house.'

But none of the lips, the tongue or the teeth will co-operate. Ferdie flicks through the pages of his newspaper. It will be added to the pile. At first, when Ferdie brought his newspapers up from downstairs I had thought he had been a journalist, or a researcher, or a writer, before the drink ensnared him. But it was merely what the psychiatrists would have called a fetish. And what I would have called laziness and lack of imagination. He was at a loss what to do with such a collection. In those papers you could have read of the declaration of World War Two. I suggested once he should offer them to a library, but that brought a curl to his lips, and he'd taken money from the tin and got drunk, returning with another newpaper under his arm.

In the draught snaking under the door and over my bed, my breast – the uncovered one – is growing cold. I cover it. I wish Ferdie would talk to me, but since that fateful morning when I suffered the stroke, he has talked to me less and less. I suppose he thinks there's no point when I can't reply with any sense. He is clearing his throat and scratching his head. Great flakes of dandruff flutter to the blankets. I wonder what the time is. I wonder what Ferdie will do when I die.

'Someone married me,' Ferdie says suddenly. 'But she took off.'

I won't take off, Ferdie, I'm thinking. His eyes look soulful in the dim light. He pats my leg.

'I think she took off with another fella. I wasn't any good with money.'

I've given Ferdie all my money. And three days before my stroke I made him a signatory for my bank account so that he could withdraw my pension. The golden girl who came from social welfare didn't like that. She liked that story the least and didn't understand when I explained that I didn't have much to start off with. At least, after my trip. Yes – although I may seem very sedentary and stationary now as I lie in my own soil – I have seen the world. Or much of it.

Nearly twenty years ago I retired, leaving those blue-blazered and vacuous girls for some other unfortunate but no doubt naively determined woman and returned to England. I visited my family and friends, those who remembered me, and sat in a budget coach with people my own age throughout the Continent. They were mostly women, mainly widowed or divorced, and although we made many jokes about geriatrics and ancients and relics, or rather I did, there was a sadness in many of them as they spoke of how Harold or Stan or Reg would have enjoyed the trip. Being a spinster with no such dead man dragging at my soul I no doubt had a better time than most, and even managed a fleeting affair with an elderly man in Florence misnamed a bellboy. None of the other dears knew about it, except for an American lady called Mavis who shared my room.

'Where have you been, Edna?' she asked, as I returned from the linen room after a night of arthritic erotica among the scratchy towels. And I didn't tell her, just as I imagine Luchio didn't tell his wife. It's true what they say about Italian men, by the way, and it would be nice to tell Ferdie, or someone, about it now. In the telling of stories one can relive the actual event. As it is, the memory of Luchio's warm hands, calloused from carrying decades of suitcases, filled with the loneliness of women of all kinds, will be mine forever.

I gain Ferdie's attention by prodding him with my right foot, then point with my right arm at where the light should be. I am concerned that he will lose his eyesight, reading in this almost dark room. He looks at me with something resembling affection and slides off the bed. He must be in a good mood tonight. The tallest column in the centre of the room begins to waver as Ferdie attempts to pick it up, away from the bulb. The shadow passes in front of him and reaches out with something resembling an arm, although its outline disappears in the grey air and pushes the teetering pile with one sharp gesture. Ferdie cries out, and I raise myself on my one good arm as the newspapers crash to the floor, burying poor Ferdie, whispering and shouting their tales of misery and disaster and fear, drowning out whatever Ferdie may have wanted to say to me before he disappeared. Try as I might I can't see him. The shadow turns to me and shows a row of white teeth. It draws closer, and I see it has the shape of a woman. She looks very proud of herself, and sits on the edge of the bed. There is something very familiar about her – the way she holds her head and drapes her long legs.

'Where did you come from?' I ask her, the instinct to make speech not easily forgotten after eighty years, even though one may not be understood. But she understands me straight away, and I am astounded. To my ears the question was clear and crisp, my English mistress voice.

She points at the newspapers.

'From there,' her voice is strange, breathy, as if she herself hasn't used it for a long time.

'How did you get in here?' I ask suspiciously.

'From between the pages. I slipped out.'

'How? Why?'

'Oh,' there is a windy laughter in her voice, 'I was tired of sitting about. I knew my destiny was to start a fire, or embrace a warm mound of fish and chips, or blow about a pavement on a wet street. In here, I felt useless.'

She may have been waiting for a long time, but she is just like the girl with the golden cross, young and impatient.

'Why were you there in the first place?'

I notice she has very little on. Just a pair of knickers made out of leopard skin.

'Can't you guess?'

She is, of course, one of Ferdie's page-three girls.

'Where is Ferdie?'

She sighs, gets up from the bed, and picks out one of the many newspapers carpeting the floor. As she returns to me, all the other columns follow suit of the tallest one now felled and descend to the floor. One pile falls across my calves, pinning me down, and another just misses my head. The page-three girl is showing me a faded photograph – Ferdie in a leopard skin G-string, draped across the bonnet of a sports car. He is not looking out of the photograph with the usual page-three coquettish smile, but staring with amazement at his huge and exposed breasts. The collage, because surely that is what it is, is so ridiculous it makes me laugh. The girl puts the newspaper down and picks her way to the door where Ferdie's jacket is hanging. She puts it on.

'Be seeing you,' she says.

The next morning there is a knock at the door. I begin to call out, to ask them in, but the power of speech miraculously restored to me the previous night, has now just as miraculously disappeared. They come in anyway – the golden girl, the more senior official, and an ambulance man.

'What's been going on in here?' demands Golden Girl, knee high in rank newsprint.

The ambulance man clears my bed of paper, and wraps me in a sheet so that in the execution of carrying me down the stairs he will not soil his uniform.

'What a fearful stink,' says Senior Official, striding to the window, now clearly visible and opening it.

'Say goodbye to all this,' says Ambulance Man, holding me in his arms at the door. I do quietly, with a tear so huge it smarts my eye. It is at the thought of never seeing Ferdie again.

'There's nothing to her,' says Ambulance Man to Senior Official.

'The old bastard must've been starving her.'

In the ambulance with Golden Girl and Senior Official following us in a government car, I contrive to die. I simply hold my breath and close my right eye. Ferdie stands in front of me, his arms outstretched, and with him Luchio, and innumerable boys in shorts. As a young girl with my head full of poetry I go to join them. It's easy really. As easy as letting a homeless man share my room in exchange for company and a dependence I chose myself.

Ania Walwicz

she was told in my red sails book in sweden a long time ago that red sails will come into my harbour they told my little girl that red sails will come with true love mister true love to me i am told now that red sails are about to enter when i am all ready for when she is grown up red sails will appear for sure it will happen exactly like that i tell now in my book that red sails are about to come very soon and very soon any day now and any day then i will be mister true then i will be mister true to me i will be mister true love i will become true true to me mister true love to me i will be mister true love my only only and no other to me told her that red sails will appear come over horizon line i know that red boat is on its way it won't be long it gets closer and closer closer than ever i'm very near nearly ready but not quite yet not just i'm not quite you know but very soon any day and any very nearly nearly my true love mister i'll come over i'll be true i'll get over i'll come to me i'll come to i'll be my true love red boat love i just have to wait and i wait my red boat is on its way i trust i hope she was told in sweden a long time ago they told my little girl that when i'm all grown up and ready for when it's all over a red sail boat will come into my harbour and i'll become mister true to me i'll be mister true true mister love to me i'll be my one and only only red sails will sail around the world to come to me why don't you come to me come to me i'm ready for nearly nearly but you know i'm not quite yet i'm not quite steady i'm harbour and i wait for me to come true to me to be my true love and no other and i wait she was told in sweden in my book that when she is all grown up and ready for when i'm alright and fully fully red sails will appear i know that it will exactly like that it gets near and near nearly there when i'm ready ready and fully

i'll be true to me i'll be mister true love and i wait come to me why
don't you come to me and i wait i'll be true love to me i'll be true
love mister love me i will be my true and only one i'll be mister true
love to me i just wait red sails come i'm nearly nearly almost there
almost but not quite and i wait when will i come i just have to wait
believe me it will any day very soon red sails are gets closer to me
nearer and nearer closer than ever just a touch but not yet red sails
will come when i'm ready for when i'm fully fully when i'm all
alright and i'm not quite quite i just wait and see red sails will appear
then i'll be mister true love to me i'll be true to me then i'll meet
me i'll be my one and only one to me i'll be true red sails about to
enter and about to i am harbour and i wait i have to trust my story
book told my little girl to wait till i'm all grown up and ready for
when i'm fully fully when it's all over this boat will come with red
sails on then i'll turn true love to me then i'll be my true mister true
love and i wait red sails just around the corner in sweden a long time
ago they told my little girl to see when i'm all grown up and ready
for red sails will arrive my i'll be true to my only only love me please
come to me i'll come true to me only then very soon just about to
and about to gets near when feels right to me i'm ready for but not
yet completely i have to wait when i'm steady level head when will
you come over red sails coming true to me i will be a meant for
longtimes i'm closer than ever i'll be true love mister red sails will
appear when i'm fully fully sure now i'll i can feel i'll be mister true
love i'll come home to me in full focus i know by ten i'm going to
sail in red sails it gets near closer and closer i'm sailor and i sail back
to me i was away i was sailing in my head i was out of me then i'll
come back to me be true sailor mister love me do i'm nearly ready
for but i'm not quite there just wait till level head then i'll be real
for steady i'm about to and about to and not yet i'm nearly there but
not yet not quite i'm almost almost and i wait

Erotic as Anything

Merrilee Moss

What am I doing? Thinking. Just thinking. Just lying here. Thinking. What? Well, yes. I do feel a bit erotic. Oh. 'The Erotic'. Yes I feel that too. Of course. Lying here alive and curled inside flesh. My flesh. Your flesh. Anyone's flesh. Particularly my own flesh. Erotic. Look. Breast to breast. All alone resting here with my breasts. I need rest because of all the fucking . . .

Sorry. All right. I'm alone. Presumably at peace and presumably erotic. (I said that already.) Nothing to do with fucking. I feel erotic because of the 'The Erotic' being a part of everything. That better?

Pudding (this belly) lies heavy along thighs hugged close. Skin (my skin) stretches taut from the base of buttocks to the tip of my neck. The sun tilts gently and appropriately over the bed. Arms, slightly burnt, squash tits into cushions which cuddle my chin. (I'm getting the idea.) It's perfect. But for the flannelette sheets. Far too knobby.

Yes. Despite the sheets I'm relaxed enough to close my eyes. Yes. I see scarlet visions of sun-filled windows. (Is that right?) Yes. I'm relaxed enough to breathe. Relaxed enough to dream. Ready?

Charlotte lies on her bed tucking her small feet under last night's pile of bedclothes. Ten years old and obviously in love. She gazes from her window. Waiting. Yearning in fact. It is dusk and deep green. Waiting for dark. A small candle (perhaps a kerosene lamp) glows by her bed. Anticipation flushes her skin. All is still.

Suddenly, her eyes widen. She draws breath. I draw breath. (Do you?) Her chest swells. There. See. Red hair. Thin face. Freckles. A long nightgown. Quick flick of white leg. Karen jumps at the window, lands briefly beside the bed, gathers Charlotte in her arms,

132

lines her face softly and quickly with kisses: neck to ear; neck to nose; neck to lips. Ah. Warm sliding lips to lips darting her tongue into Charlotte's mouth before plunging again from the window and into darkness.

Oh. The thrill of it all. Do you feel it? Anticipation. The fevered mood. If you come again tomorrow you can watch Charlotte take her turn. She will risk the wrath of parents and creep through the hydrangeas, past the silver birch . . . In the meantime Charlotte is left alone. She slips her thumb into her mouth a memory of her lover's tongue, slides her other hand between her legs . . .

Off! You're kidding. You think that's off! It's not all fantasy, you know. Part memory. Reality. I did that sort of thing. Dreamed that sort of thing. Truly. Still do. I could tell you some of my dreams . . . Much more theatre playing in this skull.

Okay. I'm listening. Still all alone here. Enjoying (trying to) 'The Erotic'. I can do it. More indirect. (She wants it more indirect.) What about simple tickling. No sex. No perversion. Definitely erotic. You'll love it.

Light fingers bouncing on air. Stroking the veins of my throat. I will choke. (I know.) On the edge of death the edge of a tickle a chuckle. Veins pop to the surface for more that's an artery under there. Be careful! I am still. Taut. Terrified blood will burst. Terrified she will stop and my flesh will be merely flesh again. From the jaw slowly slowly creeping over and over to the edge of an arm and back again. Repeat. Gentle. Erotic. See.

My throat itches. Poised waiting for her short lesbian fingernails to tear open my neck to scratch it. SCRATCH IT! Lips teeth begin to part nose pulling towards eyes tongue protruding pointing flapping about. About to scream. A contorted breathless soundless face on the edge of a scream. At this point I am totally mindless. Please. (I am victim, begging.) Please bite slice hammer your way in dig tunnels from my toes anything but stop this scream!

She does. She who has all power rejects my neck entirely leaving me frozen crippled a discarded mask surprised at its own expression unable to reconcile agony with pleasure unable to crack creases from flesh now turned to plaster. She moves slowly barely touching fingers to millimetres of space above my skin marking now a tattoo over my back.

What? Excuse me? I was busy. You don't like that either? But. Pornographic? A simple tickle. Well, I don't know. I'm rather fired by the notion of victim. My cunt swells. Direct me. Use me. This background of tears pushed past from birth forced into the sound of the sea and the immense desire/love/urge to put all of me at the feet of a beautiful woman. (Don't you feel it?) Thump. Whack. Here I am, a lump a your feet. Take that and mould it. (Please.)

Damn you. How can you see a simple tickle that way? I'll give you 'The Erotic'. (Much) more than a full moon. More than a movement of moths in wind. Feel this! Listen. Map this with your tongue.

Floods from the cunt a puddle in the bed. (You say you heard it spurt? No wonder with your ear right there.) Touching tongues. Seeking tongues. Moist lips of your face dividing. Spit mixing as brandy and dry scotch followed by beer the best of port after coffee. Filling. My hand? It is between us dragging at soft curls and padded flesh now also parting to acres of warm wet and straining vulva making waves quiver stabbing electric swords bright red from cunt to mouth and back again. You want me. (Being astute, I can tell.) Quick. I push your pelvis with my hand. From inside. Towards the roof. A ceiling rose. At the same time I eat the inside of your mouth. You are mine. I have always possessed you. I want you like this. Always available. Kneel at my feet succumb/lose control/be overwhelmed/I know you better than you know yourself.

You're fighting it. (Again.) Sorry. Teasing. But you were there. I felt you. How about some more tickling. (Yawn.) Here. It's yours.

She lifts an arm and props it with the other making a crane her forearm hanging from the elbow dangling over my back trailing without effort. Stripes on tingling flesh patterned painting an ordered shield on a body for dancing, leaving a portion untouched around my right shoulder-blade. Dead flesh. Artist fingers what about this bit? You play a game repeating that same pattern. Fingers from spine to waist spine to waist (I have never had a waist) lower and lower. But what about my right shoulder-blade?

By the time she got there it was pure orgasm. Forget the clit. Like it? Just two women, one back, several fingers and a game. Erotic as anything. A shoulder-blade.

Huh? Yes. There are erotic events/things/scenes etc. outside the bedroom. I know that. Now what are they again . . . A bit corny. I'm embarrassed. Oh. Well. Beaches. I find beaches erotic. A bit. Everything? No. I don't find everything erotic. Couldn't be. Government wouldn't allow it. What of the typewriter/conveyor belt/kitchen sink . . . No. Perhaps daisies flat open purple undersides orange sepals chanting ohm before the parallel sun, but you can't tell me scum around the bathtub is the glory/thick passion of a woman's lust! No. Definitely not. And I don't get to the beach that often.

So. What about this? In the bush. The voyeur in the bush. (Wait for it. It's different. Outside the bedroom.) Both as naked as the soil. I stand on the trunk of a low divided gum. Between branches. Feeling the bark on my skin. (Bark. Not fingers.) She (a short plump woman several metres away) is pissing squatted leaning against a tree white on grey. I watch her sway over the long grass tickling wiping flaps clear of urine before standing sun streaked and staring. I tense leg muscles to balance my breasts moving under her gaze. I watch from a great height. Soft hairs rise from her skin. Beads of sweat form and glisten. My eyes rove between sun spots. She focuses simply unmoving, staring at my pubic hair. (It's all right. We are separate.) Thick rope pulls flame to my throat. I inspect her body. (Among the trees.) Drink stillness and the heavy weight of breasts I want to suck. Each nipple hardens. (Little gum-nuts.) Our eyes drift up and down. It is midday. (Timeless like Hanging Rock.) We lower our foreheads and glare. Begin the looking again. Very equal. Very erotic.

And speaking of the country. What of watching from train windows the memory of exchanged lust in every paddock corner. Australia (you fuckin' beaut) rolling past. The buffet-car stool tiny under my throbbing belly. Outside (a natural erotica) earth heaving itself in the lustful curves of time. Making out all day and night over decades centuries universes and forever with tree roots sheep shit rivers the stars up above . . .[1]

Obsessed? Oh, come on. Admit you'd love to look up at me naked in a tree. Your skin is changing colour. I can see. Yes. I am getting carried away. Come with me. Try to get behind where I am coming from.

Your cunt is so tidy tucked up closed all flaps in despite your thrown legs. I venture close a slightly wobbly line pink brown dark brown curls that's all. Unlike me. So open exposed often dripping. Tentative I lift one side and am drawn in to a pouring soaking throbbing cave full of secrets. Mm. Superdyke flies through the sky selling icecream. Vanilla chocolate rum and raisin coffee strawberry mint and scarlet. Mm. Black aniseed with cherries perhaps.

I lie beside you watching tele. Slide down lift your shirt pull out a breast with two hands happy to have such bulk. I lick at it crawl in circles lap it warm no hurry and settle to slow sucking. Occasionally you adjust your breast for comfort, ignoring me (I love it when you ignore me). I doze your nipple resting on my lower lip.

Yes. Carried away again. But I am forever looking up or down. I love to be taken up taken in taken to Paris taken over anything, but being human, taken. Overwhelmed by the search for form. Overpowered. Teach me the way to my cunt. Or I'll teach you. Think of the relaxation. The ease. The gratitude. Admit it, you dag.[2] Or perhaps you'd like me to crawl adoring to your toes and kiss humbly all around the dirty bits.

Okay. Sorry. I apologise. I give up. I'm listening. Alone in my flannelette sheets. Alone but for the sun. (And you.) Yes. It's erotic.

The beach. Okay.

But don't you want to hear about drugs? Lying above below top to toe stoned white light flashes suspended here after the scream of flesh held in the knowledge of night morning and several hundred moods followed and filled by moments and marijuana floating dreaming spinning as the old women clap white light flashes strobe from all veins at once.

You don't? Okay. Do you know that I have often been in love with my mother.

You don't want to know?

The beach. Okay.

I walk onto the sand the music winds ecstatically into crescendo. (You like it! It gets better.) A soprano wobbles staccato then swoops into deep treble. A large brown seagull suspends in the wind. I walk onto the sand. It is cold or hot. Cold. Sleet drums blood to cheeks in gusts. Hot. Sun drives scarlet. Hands glow no matter what. Legs shiver. (Nature again in the raw.)[3] The tide is usually out. I jump between shells/rocks. Black crewcut weed glimmers as rain on leather. Puddles of sound. The music takes on a jolly note. No one at the beach. No one at the beach. No one at the beach. (Refrain.)

I am at this point a movie. Sunshine rain love story alone with my pulse. I lean on a lone pylon and stare worn wood to the sea. Circles of sand and I find a centre. Soft cream on an icy/warm sea. I breathe out. Close of opera. Hint of a rainbow amongst thick mist. Some fool trying to sail. Mostly just me and my thighs. My blood. Hot skin.

(And you.)

Far out and groovy. What's next?
Will you kneel or shall I?

1. Romance. A contrived phenomenon involving such things as 'stars up above', blurred vision and music. In this case simply nature being practical/lustful/normal.
2. A term of affection. Gentle endearment.
3. An instance of true 'eros' having been divided from our erotic continuum by the patriarchy which seeks to destroy all of nature and natural walking on beaches, placing it alongside instant sex/ potato and heterosexuality.

CALLISTEMON

Jill Golden

Lethargic, heavy, aching,
in mid-morning
I take time
                    to watch
the callistemon
                    flower in my garden.
Blood-red brush-threads
each knobbed with palest yellow
spike from cups finger-tip size,
triple-spiralled
around an inner core.

Near brush-end
green-pink skin of buds
curves smooth and whole.

At the ripening point
one tight-clenched whorl
crouches under star-shape
breaking open:
a silent slow unfurling energy,
coiled threads
splitting into crimson;
like the coil in the pit of my belly
as I wait for the bleeding.

PREMENSTRUAL

Terry Whitebeach

Angry. Irritable. Shaken by spasms of grief. Bile in my throat as I confront the voice of the self-hater. Things have stifled and constrained me for as long as I can remember. I can't bear it, must break free. It's no good talking to me of cosmic rhythms, I'm battered by cross-currents, drowning where the wild rivers meet. This going with my body is like a dance in the dark on a cliff edge. I do not want to know, do not want to see so clearly, do not want to want so passionately. Wish to mute my voice, quell the passion, be grateful for the mediocre, forget the unknown, stay safe.

The trees outside my window show luminous leaves, red-green and golden. Sunlit patterns flicker over them. I am drawn into the mystery of energy flowing into the trees and out through the leaves.

My belly is swollen. There is a ripe, ready feeling in my body, some urgent need to enfold, encompass, take into myself. The feeling frightens me. I am afraid of the responsibility and the vulnerability.

David is staying with me. I am quite crazy, I tell him. We have fought all the previous night, cataloguing our hurts, touching the wounds, sometimes gently, sometimes with great violence. We do not know where to go from here, our friendship is breaking apart. We cling to each other and sleep for a few hours in the early morning. I am so full of feelings but I cannot tell what they are. I am tired of thinking. I have two choices, to stay curled up in this foetid little nest and follow this craziness through to its end or to move outward to the work of preparation.

I choose the latter. I'm sick of this sweaty bed, smelling of fear and pain and stale night-time breaths and bodies. So I weed the garden, do the washing, clean the house and cook more food than we can eat: filling bellies, cleaning the nest, it's all part of the need to create order and calm. I light incense sticks as I plod about the house in my bulky body.

In the evening I go out to the book discussion group and argue passionately against the things that keep us separate, against the violence of order and stability. We walk home slowly in the dark. Gwen is very breathless, her recent heart operation has made walking difficult for her, but the doctor has told her to walk a lot and so she does.

David has remade the bed with fresh sheets. He has added an extra mattress so that the bed is soft and enfolding, all feathers and pillows and fluffy covers. We flop into it, exhausted. We do not fight, do not talk, just breathe each other's breath and try to push the ten-ton cat off our feet. We search for the warmth of each other, and, finding it, sleep.

I have been in the bush and seen seed-cases exploding. Round. Plump. Full. Then springing open with a crack! Seeds scattering. Received by the earth. Once, at Pathways, I squatted so that I could bleed onto the earth. I watched my blood seep into the dark leaf mould and then I rubbed my cunt on the warm damp ground. It was a good feeling.

We both stir. Will we argue again? Please not, we are both too sleepy, too comfortable. I feel a stirring in my body: will it cause me to cry out against the things I am allowing to strangle me or will it lead me deep into the labyrinth to the root of my troubles? I cannot know, there is no certainty anymore. David is murmuring and snuggling closer. I feel his inner arm against my breast, I focus on that feeling. My breasts ache, they are heavy. He puts his hand on my belly, a little afraid.

My blood sings. This is the place of choices: to go deep into the silence, to be still and heavy and pregnant with waiting? To engage in struggle to flush the daemons out into the open; or to follow the song of the blood that is beating in our heads? We make our choice.

We have always been muddled by the mechanics of sex, by the etiquette, the manners. Of how to accommodate the penis when the consciousness feels lesbian, of who is male and who is female. We have felt the paradoxes so strongly, sometimes losing ourselves in them, sometimes celebrating them, fierce and tender, empty and full, giving and receiving.

'Yes . . . yes . . . yes,' David murmurs as we stroke each other. It's our ritual to banish fear, to make us willing to enter the dark, to cast into limbo, to feel the power and to unleash it in each other. A wide and fertile place, with no boundaries, the very threat and promise of freedom.

Last night we looked for a while into the Starhawk book and David laughed when I curled up in pleasure at the image of the wolf fangs. Now wolf-woman comes to me, I hear her long, wild howling in this dark red place, and I surrender to the feel of her hot breath; fur, fangs, limbs intertwined. She sings us into being and the power is released. We let it have its way.

When we finally untangle ourselves, too hot to be close any longer, we laugh with delight, then sink into a peaceful, musing stillness. It's all in the blank spaces if you have the eyes to see it. In the quietness I remember a note left on my pillow a few years ago by a devoted lunatic in whose company I had loped through several lifetimes. It had read, 'You're not bad for a poufta sheila!' The acceptance and the humour of it still warm me. I don't share the memory of it with David. The body is such a secret thing sometimes, half-tamed, demanding, wild, shy and tender.

For a while we lie in comfortable silence. Then David speaks. He simply says, 'The two shall become one flesh,' and is quiet again. This confirmed sceptic, quoting the *Book of Common Prayer?* The mind baulks. The heart rejoices. I take the words deep into the cave in the centre of the labyrinth, where the power lies, and leave them there. Now all is ready. Tomorrow I will bleed.

LOVING PARENTS

Jennifer Strauss

Sometimes, night-waking, they made love
As if two strangers frantic to be known,
As if unfeaturing darkness stripped away
Affectionate disguises, long-term habits
Which daylight coupling decently assumed,
And laid the fierce nerves of loving bare.

Such times, they moved about their morning chores
Abstracted, in a sensual shadowed glow
Where suckling babies might bask mindlessly
But awkward older children, growing wise,
Looked askance, and bruised their egos' fists
Against that dark complicity which gave them being.

THE RESURRECTION OF THE BODY

Jenny Pausacker

The three of us had lunch together on an average of once a month. Neat sandy Ed – don't know if I'd recognise him in the street if I hadn't known him for fifteen years. Neil with the white streak in his wild black hair and the flamboyant gestures that toppled at least one wine glass per meal – you'd recognise him, all right, even if you'd only seen him once across a restaurant. As for me, well, I recognise myself every morning when I'm shaving. I'm told I look like a footballer, with the implication that this is unusual for an accountant.

It all started when Ed casually mentioned the latest section of the public service to be offered to private enterprise. We know each other pretty well, so Neil wasn't overreacting when he launched straight into a lecture on the need for economic rationalism. I usually leave them to it, but this time I found myself catching Neil's eye and saying, 'Well, well. I thought I was the only one who'd copped out on changing the world.'

Neil wasn't thrown – in fact, he leaned across to grip my shoulder. 'Come off it, Mick. You're no more of a cop out than I am. We've all still got the same ideals as in the old Carter Street days. Okay, I have to go along with the Department to a certain extent – I can't be a free spirit, like Ed as an Adm 7. But the way I look at it, we're a team. The Three Musketeers of the public service, right?'

'And what's my role in this team?' I persisted.

'You? You're the family man,' Ed said with his unexpected sweet smile. 'Sometimes, when I've spent two-thirds of the weekend slaving over a report, I find myself thinking, "What the hell am I doing this for?" and the short answer, every time, is, "Mick's kids.""'

'Hang about,' Neil grumbled jovially. 'Mick's not the only person in the world with kids.'

'I know, I know. But that's what I think.'

So lunch ended on a friendly note, after all. Back in the office, though, I realised that I'd actually wanted to push Neil and Ed until they had to admit that they were really poles apart these days. Why on earth would I suddenly get the urge to stir my two oldest mates? Well, the truth of the matter was that they both seemed pretty contented, in their own ways, whereas I –

The family man. For crying out loud!

That was the first time I really admitted to myself, outside of the house, that Sandy and I were having serious problems.

At first the situation had seemed fairly simple. Sandy was tired every night. *Tired.* Imagine my pen digging into the page. I'd seen her tired from broken nights with the babies, I'd seen her tired from hours of study, but this was different. The broken nights we shared together, joking and swearing and hugging and bickering our way through them. And Sandy had shared the nights of study with me in her questions or excitement or apologies. But this tiredness went beyond sharing.

I understood what she was going through, of course. I cooked a few extra meals per week, gave Tim and Vicky and Emma extra cuddles, repeated my interesting bits of news over the blare of the TV. I was so busy being understanding that it took at least a dozen weeks before I realised that there was something missing in me as well.

Actually, I don't see how I could've worked it out any sooner. I don't happen to be a necrophiliac, and in the time I took to clean my teeth every night, Sandy worked up a pretty fair imitation of a corpse. After a month or so, she would manage to open her eyes a crack and mumble an affectionate goodnight, which was an improvement, and in the morning we might even struggle into a kiss before the alarm flung us out of bed.

I wasn't exactly frustrated. Her back felt solid and warm, not tantalising or a barrier between us. Sandy has a broad back – she claims that this is what makes her an 18C, though when I crooked my arms around her, those breasts felt just as solidly warm. Knees tucked behind hers, I nestled comfortably against her broad buttocks. I wasn't carrying on about conjugal rights. I wasn't even flinging myself across the bed to jerk off with ostentatious stealthiness. It took a while for it to dawn on me that I didn't have the motivation. In other words, I hadn't had a hard on in weeks.

No problems, I thought, edging carefully away. I'll settle that statistic here and now. Sandy and I had a fairly active sex life, so this wasn't exactly routine, but it's like riding a bicycle – you never forget how. I piled up the doona a bit and dredged a hanky from the back of the bed, by which time I felt about twelve years old. I was practically looking around for the stack of tattered *Playboys* to get me going. This is bloody ridiculous, I thought, and fell asleep seconds later.

Just the same, the statistic stuck in my mind, and I kept half an eye on myself for the next few days. Point one: a stranger comes into the office – I don't check to see if she's an 18C. Point two: there's a giant ad of a woman's bum outside my window – I can't remember when it replaced the giant aerial view of a tropical island. Point three: a young girl jostles me on the train – I step aside politely. And so on. Listen, I don't want to sound as if I generally wear through my fly seams on an average of once a month, but I'm a normal bloke, whatever that means, and this wasn't my idea of normal.

Still, it wasn't dramatic enough to qualify as a problem. I could list a hundred or so things I did per day, over and above thinking about my dick. A lot of my thoughts were commonsense ones, too – thoughts about Sandy being tired, and me not getting any younger, and all the couples in the surveys who screw once a month or once a year or once in a blue moon. I also told myself I wouldn't improve matters by brooding.

So I didn't brood, right? I put it out of my mind, except that, being a bloke, I had to take a look at it five or six times a day. Anyway, I'd be shaking myself dry and sometimes my penis would sort of flop against my hand, as if it was begging for mercy. It looked like a worm, a pathetic helpless red earthworm, except that earthworms burrow through the ground and keep things moving while this was limp and useless, insignificant. Worm-like.

That's why I wanted to talk to Ed and Neil, though I couldn't exactly see myself butting into a discussion of the socialist left to say, 'Hey, fellers, my dick looks like a worm. What can I do about it?' So instead I sat in my office and stared into the window of my calculator.

That weekend Sandy came back to life a bit. We'd been for a walk along the beach, with Tim and Vicky and Emma churning up the sand in all directions or racing back to show us the latest bit of shell or dead jellyfish. Scrambling over red brown rocks, Sandy and I held hands, and our grip grew tighter as we herded the kids back along the orange shore. Her cheeks still glowed from the wind as she leaned back on the pillows. Long liquid kisses. I kept hoping she'd put her hand on my cock in the proprietorial way she has sometimes. I felt very close to her. We snuggled deeper into each other's bodies. Later on, she'd say something like, 'I'm really sorry I'm so tired, Mick. It'll be better soon.' Or she'd thank me for being so patient. But that night we simply floated into sleep, clasped tight.

Next day I tried something I'd been considering for a while, partly in the interests of my own personal research, partly because on the whole happily married men don't hang around sex cinemas, so I was curious to see whether the standard of porn had changed much since my younger days. I found a Thrust Cinema well away from the office and strode in, pretending to myself that I was a researcher from *Choice*. In the company of five other men I sat patiently while two girls patted each other gingerly, then started to moan for no observable reasons. For a while I tried to cheer myself up by working out how the place could possibly run at a profit, given city rentals and audiences of six, but in less than quarter of an hour I found myself striding back up the aisle, thoroughly depressed by a tedious sequence of couples removing their clothes and their inhibitions together. I suppose the management made a clear profit from me, at least.

Funnily enough, that night the worm lifted its head and sniffed the air. It wasn't the memory of the film, it was the memory of myself watching that excited me.

Not enough, though. I preferred to sleep.

I take the train to work every morning. Beyond rectangles of thick glass the city slides past. Outside, people are running for buses, delivering mail, dropping off their kids at school or opening shops, but I'm separate from all that.

I always thought impotence would be an active matter, like the little engine they told us about at kindergarten – 'I think I can, I can.' I always thought – no, for Christ's sake, I never thought I would be impotent, but I would've assumed I'd be off my brain, rushing to doctors, worrying endlessly, my sense of manhood threatened. Instead of watching, through thick glass, my own bewildering placidity.

That morning a colleague dropped in to my office. He could hardly stand still, always darting over for another look at the bum outside my window. 'Jesus, Mick, how'd you be, a thing like that hitting you in the face every time you look up? It's a wonder you ever get any work done,' and so on.

I knew what I was supposed to say, but I didn't even bother to try, because no way in the world could I have managed the glint in the eye to go with it. Luckily the bum's admirer was too wound up to notice, but all the same I was worried, and as we sat down to lunch I blurted out, 'Ed, what do you do if the blokes at work are, y'know, talking about sex and expecting you to join in?'

His pale eyes sharpened. 'They *don't* expect me to.'

Then Neil appeared, demanding to know what we were talking about and immediately launching into a denunciation of sexual harassment in the workplace. Afterwards, of course, I realised that I'd managed to say exactly the wrong thing. Not to mention messing up my chances of bringing up the subject again in the right way.

Mind you, I didn't really expect my old mates to come up with some kind of five-point plan for me. If I'd been wanting answers, I could've easily gone and looked myself up in a medical textbook, I suppose, but I still didn't think of it as permanent, especially since it didn't really bother me. When Sandy started to make longer apologies, I quite openly admitted that I hadn't been that interested in sex myself lately. 'You?' she said, laughing, and she put her hand on my cock in that proprietorial way she has sometimes. I noticed with no sense of threat that she was stroking the worm's back, lightly brushing its head. Then, without any warning, she went wriggling around, sending the doona flying. Her mouth engulfed me.

I did my best, but all the time my brain kept chanting, 'Why now? Why now?' It would have been fine, any of those nights when we held each other closely, but right now, when we'd just been talking about what *wasn't* happening . . . and I don't think anyone finds it that easy to talk about sex. Oh, I knew Sandy meant well, but that isn't always enough. So, seconds before I had to fight my way free, I said, keeping my voice even, 'Looks like it's my turn to be too tired.' We kissed amiably, our bodies tucked together, and fell asleep easily, with no more discussion.

Or so I hoped, but in fact Sandy had efficiently put me on the agenda for discussion at the next meeting. The moment I heard that we'd hired a sitter and made a booking at the birthdays-and-celebrations restaurant, I knew exactly what I was in for. I talked a marathon that night. I was so witty and entertaining that I ended up with stomach cramps. And that's all I got out of my brilliant strategy, because in the end Sandy went off to the dunny, sidled back well out of my sight lines and said at the exact moment her bum hit the chair, 'Micky, are you threatened by my job?'

Frankly, I found that pretty offensive. Feminism was in the air already when I was in my early twenties, so I've been breathing it for a decade. I cook, I help with the kids, I'm not a slob around the house – for Christ's sake, I was the one who suggested Sandy should go back to uni. But no, one little thing goes wrong, and instantly I'm the original big bad wolf.

What's more, in this nice neat accusation popping out of nowhere, I was sure I could hear echoes of girl talk. Fair enough, no man can ever be a hundred per cent sure of what women talk about among themselves, but I've lived with a woman for eleven years (or thirty-four years if you count my mother and sister) and I think I've got a pretty good idea.

'It's your job, Sandy,' her friends would have said. 'Men always feel threatened when you start to do as well as them.'

I didn't say any of this, though. I just murmured, very gently, 'Sandy,' and waited to see if she was prepared to back it up. After a while I added, just as gently, 'What on earth put that idea into your head?'

She finished cutting a new potato into tiny pieces before she said, 'Well, we've never really talked about the fact that we're both working in the public service now . . .' and she switched to chasing a snow pea through a slick of sauce.

'Sandy,' I repeated. 'We're not even in the same department, let alone the same line of work. We're hardly going to find ourselves competing for promotion. Though even if we were,' I added sincerely, 'I reckon we could talk it through.'

She mumbled something about it being stupid and just an idea, then held up her glass to catch the light, as if we really were celebrating. I couldn't seem to think of anything more to say, though, and we left soon afterwards.

One small sentence from another person, but it crashed through my protective screen like a stone, and after that I couldn't stop myself from thinking. Not that it did me much good. I mean, Sandy had worked before, and our sex life was fine then. All right, this was a much better job, but no better than mine. Her salary was lower than mine at the moment, but I can't say I wanted to chuck a nervo at the idea that she might draw even over the next few years. In fact, with three kids headed for private schools, I hoped she would. No matter how hard I tried to believe I was jealous of Sandy's success (and in a way it would've been a relief to have some kind of answer, even that one), I couldn't make it ring true. I like my work and I'm good at it; I wouldn't have thanked anyone who tried to give me Sandy's job instead.

By now I was so desperate that I rang Neil and suggested lunch. After we'd ordered, I cleared my throat and said 'By the way, I remember you saying that you'd decided to go and see a shrink. How did that work out?'

Neil lit up like a fluorescent tube. For the next three-quarters of an hour he explained that he'd hated his older brother because he could always make their parents laugh. This had given Neil a compulsive drive for achievement, which in turn created stress, but now he felt much more of a whole person. As we were leaving, he turned to me and said, 'Funny, I never thought you or Ed would be interested in hearing all of this. Really, Mick, you should try it yourself some time.'

I smiled noncommittally and decided I'd rather be impotent.

Impotent.

Impotent.

Once I started to put a name to it, everything seemed so much more serious. Or rather, when Sandy started to put a name to it, as she kept trying to do, mainly when we were in bed together. Granted, we could hardly chat about our sexual problems in front of Tim and Vicky and Emma. Things were bad enough without our becoming the main feature at Show and Tell time. Still, I found the whole business quite upsetting. I was lying in bed one night, wishing that I could stop Sandy's breathing – she had started to wheeze asthmatically again – when suddenly she let out a yelp and sat bolt upright.

'Bad dream, sweetheart?' I mumbled, making my voice sound drowsy.

She sat and shivered for a moment, then her hand snaked across and touched my shoulder lightly.

'Oh Micky, I'm so scared,' she whispered. 'I really love my work, but I don't want to lose you. What's happening to us?'

So now we were even having heart-to-hearts in our sleep. 'If you must know,' I said bitterly, 'I've never been the least bloody threatened, but the fact is that ever since you got that fucking job, I might as well be shacked up with one of the blokes from the office, for all the good it does me.'

Silence. Then through the darkness drifted the ghost of a chuckle. 'Truly, Mick? Do I really feel like one of the blokes from the office?'

As we snuggled deeper into each other's bodies, I had to admit that she didn't. She floated into sleep, clasped tight.

But I lay there, staring out at the darkness beyond her broad warm back, horrified at what I had just said. I'm not anti-gay. I don't even think that gays are especially talented and creative, I just think they're people. Ed's a great guy, and I'd let my brother marry him like a shot, if you see what I mean. So why was I suddenly using the idea of sleeping with a bloke as the ultimate put-down? I could see the answer very clearly and then, it felt like a few seconds later, the alarm went off.

I was on my way home from the station when I remembered my great revelation from the night before. It was a bit more embarrassing in broad daylight, but I still had to admit that, the time Sandy started to go down on me, I'd reacted as if I'd found a bloke about to do the same thing. Thanks, but no thanks. I had to stop and check that the milkbar was still securely anchored on the corner, the sky was still blue. But they were, and I was repeating over and over, 'She's not better than me, she's the same as me, the same as me. And I'm a man.'

All along I'd been convinced that if I could just work out what was causing the problem, then I'd instantly have the cure for it – like Sandy, when the nerves and bronchitis she'd believed in for years were re-diagnosed as asthma, and they gave her a spray, and she sprayed away the night-time chokings. No such luck for me, though. I wasn't gay.

Anyway, I knew Sandy wasn't a man. And I definitely didn't want to end the marriage. Taking Tim and Vicky and Emma to the zoo once a week didn't exactly appeal, and besides, whatever was going on between Sandy and me, I still seemed to love her. I always wanted to kiss her when she got home or when I got home. We always had something to say, and a laugh or two. Things were only difficult for half an hour before bedtime and half an hour after.

So, all right, my great revelation had been and gone, leaving everything pretty much the same as before. I went to work, I had lunches with Neil and Ed, I played with the kids, Sandy and I were very polite to each other at bedtime, and it seemed as if we could go on that way for the rest of our lives.

Finally one night I walked in to find Sandy and the kids parked in front of the TV, Sandy knocking back neat gin with a very determined look. It's an indication of my state of mind by then that I instantly assumed that lack of sex had sent her round the twist. Of course, it turned out to be nothing to do with me. I won't go into the whole story, but the upshot of it was that Sandy's boss had taken a report she'd really slaved over and slammed it in no uncertain terms *and* in front of the whole office. After I'd sympathised for a while, I went out and got four pizzas, which made it a red letter day in the kids' eyes. Sandy cheered up too, and in the end it was a pretty good evening all round.

Such a good evening that a few unexpected thoughts were beginning to cross my mind, and when Sandy threw herself on me the moment I climbed into bed, I felt more than willing. It was a few seconds before I realised that she wasn't exactly shaking with lust; the poor kid was in tears. I wasn't disappointed, I was happy to comfort her, and so I was stroking her hair and listening to her run through the whole thing again when she gulped and said angrily. 'He never would've spoken to Dan like that. It's because I'm a woman.' I went on stroking her hair, then her breasts, murmuring, 'Poor baby' and 'want me to go and beat him up?' She started to giggle, and kissed me hard, and suddenly there was nothing to worry about, no parts and bits and thoughts and doubts, just me and Sandy rocking together and gasping together and moving apart for a second and then coming together, the way it had always been.

I went out to the bathroom, I was singing while I pissed. 'The trumpets shall sound, and the dead shall be raised incorruptible.' We did bits of the *Messiah* for my school speech night, but I tell you, I never knew what that line meant before. 'The trumpet shall sound,' I told Sandy and we were at it again. She held my cock, how could I have called it a worm? It was raised incorruptible. 'And we shall be saved,' that's what Handel said – or the Bible, I suppose. Well, we were saved. By a fluke, yes. By no intention of our own, yes. By fairly dubious circumstances, yes, I'd have to admit that. But it was worse before, and better afterwards. Surely that has to count for something.

The whole world looked better to me. I whistled my way to my desk, and learned that half the office believed I'd had a virus the last few months. They were glad to see me looking my old self, and I was glad to take a look at my new self. I strode into the restaurant at lunchtime, wondering if Ed and Neil would notice any difference, but they were deep in a discussion of AIDS. As Neil asked his tenth searching question, I realised I was having the unusual experience of seeing Ed embarrassed.

'Listen,' he said finally, 'I know this must sound incredibly irresponsible. Let me assure you, I have been reading articles in the gay press for years, and I should be able to define safe sex in minute detail for you, but – well, the fact is that for the last few years I've been having the safest sex imaginable.' He coughed, 'That is to say, none at all.'

'Don't you miss it?' Neil asked involuntarily.

'Not exactly.' He coughed again. 'I've really got into my book on the Labor Party. And there's the job, my friends – I run for an hour every day – I don't have *time* for lovers.'

Now that he'd explained himself, the pink receded from Ed's ears, and he looked across alertly at us, interested to see what we would make of this. Neil was already flinging his hands up.

'God, if I could only feel that way! I'm in such a mess at the moment. I'm having an affair with Julie, our new project officer – it started soon after I went to the shrink. I know it's crazy, especially given that we work together, but it's so amazingly passionate, I'm learning so much about myself –'

'And does Diane know about it?' I asked.

'I *said* I was in a mess. She's just issued an ultimatum – oh, I can't blame her, I'd probably react the same way in her position, but –' he drifted away.

'But Julie's so great in bed?' Ed suggested with a grin.

'No, don't get me wrong, sex with Diane's still fantastic too,' Neil assured us eagerly. 'And then there's the kids, I don't see enough of them as it is. I don't want to lose Diane – I just don't want to lose Julie either. If I could just explain that I love them both, in completely different ways!'

Ed and I spontaneously started a slow handclap, and Neil swung from one to the other like a gored bull, before he laughed. 'Okay, okay. I suppose you may've heard that line before. I would've thought you could afford to be kind, though, Mick – you and your cosy little family where nothing ever goes wrong.'

I wasn't obliged to say anything. After all, there was nothing wrong, not now. I looked across at my oldest friends.

'That's all you know about,' I said. 'I've been impotent for the last eight months.'

'And now?' Ed asked politely.

'Well, yes, things've improved lately, or I probably wouldn't have got around to mentioning it,' I admitted.

'So what's your secret?' demanded Neil.

I could imply that Sandy and I discovered a long-lost footnote to the *Kama Sutra*. Or I could tell the truth. There was no doubt about which of these two possibilities was the more risky. If I told them the truth, I laid myself wide open to misinterpretation or, worse still, to being interpreted correctly and then judged. On the other hand, I'd known Ed and Neil for fifteen years. If you can't take a few risks with your old mates, then what are old mates for?

As I opened my mouth, I was still wondering what I was going to say.

THE MIRACLE HEALER

Cornelia Carman

It had rained most of the day, so that when the sun finally came out in the late afternoon it was very welcome. The sky was golden, reflected against the steel grey clouds of the receding storm. Alice decided to have a 'real' drink before dinner, instead of the usual glass of white wine. The Scotch winked at her. From the kitchen window she watched the last raindrops form on the roof of the trailer next door, a feeling of peace and well-being came over her.

She remembered yesterday and the blue heron, so unafraid that it had allowed her to approach within a yard, its beady yellow eyes seemingly oblivious to her presence; and later the anhinga, shaking its prehensile wings to dry on the mangrove branch. A feeling of oneness with the universe pervaded her and the urge to make a physical gesture suddenly swept over her. She put down the glass, slid open the door and stepped from an aluminium and formica world out on to the wet grass. The world smelled of green and wet, decaying fungus and compost.

When she arrived at the swimming pool next to the park club-house, no one was there. She slipped off her clothes as naturally as breathing. The water was luscious, warm and rippling. She swam on her back and watched the wavelets break over her erect pink nipples. Further down a dark triangle appeared and disappeared in a froth of pale blue bubbles. She rolled over and gloried in a strong kick. She was Dawn Fraser. No, she was a golden fish. She dived down and the water stroked her with gentle passion.

As she floated on her back, debris from the storm and frangipani flowers drifted past. She looked up at the bruised sky. The clouds were black galleons sailing on a purple sea. There were flashes of

154

lightning in the distance, and low rumblings. There was sunlight in the sky too, and its rays picked up ribbons of silver raindrops. While she drifted, Alice became aware of a stream of bubbles from the side of the pool. She sought its source and leaned into it. A perfect massage.

The bubbles gushed into her face, then across her shoulders and, as she turned, into the small of her back. She arched into position, so that bubbles exploded in a steady stream on her clitoris. Her grunts of pleasure turned into sighs, turned into moans. She knew that the bubbles would never stop, never tire like fingers or tongues. Finally she could resist no longer and she let the eruption come.

At her very moment of ecstasy, the wheelchair pushed around the corner of the clubhouse. In it sat a caricature of a woman. One side of her was attractive, slender and grey-haired. The other side was shrivelled and wizened, one claw clutching a cigarette. Her husband guided the wheelchair, leaning forward from time to time to remove the butt from the tightly pressed and twisted lips, insert a fresh cigarette and light it.

The chair came to an abrupt halt in front of Alice. She was spread-eagled, head tilted back, eyes closed in pleasure. The husband took refuge in the hearty approach, pretending to ignore what his eyes relayed to his brain.

'Good evening. How d'you like the rain? Are you visiting here?'

The woman said nothing. But then the miracle occurred. Her jaw dropped and her mouth, for the first time in years, gaped open, smiling.

THE SEXUALITY OF ILLUSION

Mary Fallon

I am a person, before I'm a woman and it's been a shield, this feeling. I was always a person first. I never felt female despite the church dresses in nylon and lace.

Now this woman in my life opening me up spreading me out poking tender places. I'd like to live with her all day and not say anything or move much. It's strange this sexuality discovered. It's sensuality and love and passion and frustration and tenderness and delicate. I can't believe her beauty. I feel like I am holding a soft waxy flower all night. She's like a star or a flower or a small young green tree. I want to forget my day-by-day-going-through-the-motions life when I'm with her. I see it as something I have no real involvement in. She's saving my poetry saving the soul in me. I want to fuck her and have her kiss her cunt suck her nipples hold her down rock on her body watch her smile see her cry ask her to kiss me. Lust and love, delicate moisture amazing smoothness amazing smallness like a drop of water huge and minute.

Do you think the tragedy of our lives is that we can't usually see our way out of a darkened room?

Do you think the tragedy of our lives is in their dullness, is in our dullness, our dulled minds, dulled senses, oh how-do-our-eyes-stay-open brains?

Are we going to live a decent life? Is this what we get? Are we as happy as we will ever be?

Yes I may have found a delicate balance between the tragedy, the chaos and the humour, the joy, the mystery?

No you have not. Your face is falling down I see but I must beg you to stay on top of it all see it from where you are way up there – on top.

Come back to bed. Come back to where the variables are you and me and the light through the window and the position of the blankets.

I have bought yellow and orange flowers and arranged them in a cream jam jar with maidenhair fern so there's sunlight in our room.

In the rain I feel tears I cannot cry for you. I remember poems for you. They roll around in my head and my fingers tap them out onto your stomach and thighs.

'Somewhere I have never travelled gladly beyond any experience your eyes have their silence in your most fragile gesture are things which enclose me and which I cannot touch because they are too near. Your slightest look easily will unclose me though I have closed myself you open petal by petal myself as spring opens delicately mysteriously her first rose.

'No one not even the rain has such small hands.'

I lie, I do e.e. cummings great injustice, but the rain is in it and the flower and the minute delicacy I see in you.

'Shit,' I said, 'It's not going to work. You'll never be happy like this. You'll go. I won't be able to cope.'

'No, I won't,' you said.

JUNE 1976 – SYDNEY

white burgundy and you and Saturday afternoon in the suburbs and we're at odds after harsh love-making eye locking against eye in frown and hopeless gesture is it because I like to play games and you like it simple because they're roughhanded heavy-footed games to pull sex out of you willingly/unwillingly and you want to flow along sweet kisses and smooth as darkness is it because at last we're alone with the kid gone for the weekend and we've a makeshift silent space between the walls of the suburban normality and work-a-day world and like beggars in vacant lots we bed down on each other at last but unable to bring peace out of frustration and pain we sit back tired to death and bitchy as hell with our bodies and fingers that poke and pull instead of lull and love I crave release from the impotence of being a woman in a man's world a peddler at a salesmen's convention always a dreamer I do not want to drown in the gutter of tears which separate reality from dreams so I hold you so soft a dream so substantial a reality so much mine and part of me and lover

she shakes the bed with her soft cries and moans my moan-deep soft bed of shivering cries where we sleep and love a body of dreams my dream girl fancy fantasy body magic with dream life (don't be wide-eyed about it darling)

your petal smooth Persian carpet eroticism which cloaks my garden and we are in the night all growth under the moon

and are we to wake exotic beast and bird woven into a carpet garden

APRIL 1977 – SYDNEY

there we sat by the fire trying to stoke some flame back into our dreary warm love as if too much pressure had been applied over too many years and now it was flat cold bloodless I knew but you would not believe and I tried to tell you reasonably then harshly then brutally but you only grew anxious and blaming always saying it will be good again soon and I loved your presence and your eyes so much and the child's mouth that gave so little that I gave in grew silent about the one dimensional love we had become you were my pornographic movie every day the colours of your skin the slant of your hair suggested slivers of fantasies and I concocted elixirs aphrodisiacs to increase passion from these fragments

APRIL 1978 – SYDNEY

at night I dream
   a dark circle around my heart
   two crows circling
   ringbarkedwhiteheart
   with
   I am innocent
   written all over it
   still
   tearing it out vicious
      indifferent

and during the day
>   making terrible excuses to be with you
>   wanting taxis to run all over the city
>   to you wanting to sit beside you
>   follow you everywhere with my eyes
>   your blue axe eyes having struck
>   out my heart blazing a trail
>   along my nerves
>   I lie rigid in your arms
>   exhaust myself in telling
>   too many truths
>   climb walls
>   abseiling ganglia
>   and hanging suspended

>   a waterfall trying
>   to fill a cup
>   the ocean in love
>   with an oyster
>   two marshes merging
>   a periphery of trees
>   a moon like a
>   scarred heart
>   a scoured plate

and me thinking it would come together waiting hanging out for that time and the relief and the beginning of a new period for us and me loving you as infatuated as ever wanting you so much and coming to bed and beginning to feel walls falling scales brushed off with your hands and sex opening and my heart flowering softly and crying out for you in bed and becoming a woman and having sex and orgasm straight and believing in your arms and eyes and straight talk and now you say I never really opened to you sexually what does that mean to me what does that mean it means four years of slow growth attachment and a final flowering denied it means my sexuality passion emotions denied again and again and forever we will always and forever avoid the centre of the cyclone the eye of the storm forever and always resist peace

>   we have lost each other
>   or found each other

not to be what we had imagined
I am a great fool
my mother took
old chairs and
renovated them
I take people
and rehabilitate them
emotionally
I am a crackpot eccentric
renovator of people
my mother took tools to antiques
found in wood heaps and
under old houses
I take the unwieldy tool of myself
many pronged with
my inner resources
to people

at last I am serious
no mucking about
for the first time
in many years
I am serious
I want you out

'I am never anywhere now not alone nor am I without you'

perfected
gouged out tooled into by
a curled tongue
and your craftsmans grip
on your firm words
telling me this (sawdust)
and
telling me this (sawdust)
and
telling me this (sawdust)
at the third stroke
your time is up at the third stroke
you will survive on the memory of the smell
of an oil rag

struck in the face
by
a
gesture
reminiscent of you
struck in the stream of my long long
memory and memorising by a bolt from
the blue
flotsam and jetsam

you have come up against me again
as you do
like a wet-slap-bang-in-the-face-fish
I was walking down Central Tunnel
the busker the slack offkey music
my life you in my life sad effluent
sad brown water

this is the end of love with my name on it.

Ania Walwicz

most handsome everybody wants best fresh young chief warder is after hairy lets know come over takes to his you do what takes trousers off won't any duties you be good to treat i come quick i'm by self carpets double bed help out library momma's boy i'm weak swivel little wheels he got big push over easy for favourite everyone knows what what's smooth dark sixteen maybe thirteen doe eyed in vienna wealthy leather all that silver got this brother very close dress clings walk estate park suntanned he's give me lessons gardeners chauffeurs peek through eye glasses we go out much too close get wet in unforeseen showers goodness you must take all your clothes immediately so off of course i do because otherwise i will catch awful chill sausage roll curls another brother don't get confused now he's vulgar big lapels squeaky shoes must stop car even though it's too much too late already what you stop car for when i'm on my way to my first communion dress with flounces oh dear can't about any else at moment bit rest big room bit of phoney posh she want to where is but won't ask just hold doors when she lifts i can't help it prisoner comes please hide from the police what can i do but must shower one is rounder against table couldn't just wait why you interrupt across knees must do now out because it's much too hot taking off shirts only in one room had only one bed we musn't we just relax i'm not doing any harm take it easy did you do your homework must do my homework but i'm putting it off for too long try to concentrate on pirates catch hooligans hold but fall in love all the same a muscly for nothing else now because anytime of day felt like please try pyjamas spread on urge felt touch in changing room of togs pressing very close said must come with or hide with nurse soldier he was very sick so he's in bed i'm looking after but had an accident so doesn't hadn't any and no danger you were so naughty on bottie deserve a must suck small enough on a picnic takes roll up rug tartan mohair must unrolls and kiss they seem to or sit on knees a long dress on public park bench keeping straight face with they can't see anyway backcar wants to help he comes front from seat arch on rolls he is in bed with not to hold over too long needing there wasn't even bottles in must have i've got curly on a vinyl couch can wipe it she had to anytime he wants on grass too can't hold it anymore how long to wait half an hour does it will for can pour after washbasin sitting in hand bowl while he or bowl have to watch hole in bushes a relief for deserve it rolls stockings he is in a hurry why do you wait for and the prisoner having to be tied in case i phone the police it is sordid but a kind of what mix must sweaty while she slept didn't know who orals for exams is french what are you doing next room a shock to see but won't out a fat one doorjamb stand will do anything what did you do just let me it didn't stop must have followed till what's the time please she is bathe he ask mecenas dark bald hairyback stops at no thing never only for pleasure keep secretary had have to do it very soon beach dune behind when nobody looks keyholes this is forbid leave us touch your must or no ask name or take him to his scout leaders in knee socks backyards doorways secrets pull up dresses really very pleasant when to happen in middle just had was very hadn't any so over again it's hard very hard i'm delicate workman wait a surprise about to do shopping had to relieve sit her in care of i am getting all dressed and she powder puff last minute are you going to i think so in mouth she's exhausted by now can hardly

HOW HIGH IS THE SKY?

Helen Hodgman

Aged thirty Hazel woke up and, finding she had no urgent need to pee, decided to stay in bed a while to think things over. First, though, she must secure the rattling blind. Kneeling on the bed to do this, she saw a tall Mexican in striped pyjama pants standing on a square of dead grass watering the concrete by the pool.

Only two vehicles remained in the parking lot: the Alfa, parked skewiff across two spaces; a Winebego Super Chief with the words HOGGS MIRACLE REVIVAL CRUSADES painted in red letters along its side, parked next to a huge white plaster brontosaurus with little blue lights for eyes. Inside the Winebego a woman sat watching colour cartoons on TV. Hazel thought she should take the Alfa through a carwash today and have the finishers pay particular attention to the gas stains round the gas cap.

A Chicana maid wheeled a cart piled with fresh linen and cleaning things along the first floor balcony of the facing units. She skirted the ice-machine, the bottles of cleaning fluids rattling together as she did so, and reaching the end unit above the pool. She left the trolley, stepped to the rail and stood a moment looking down on the Mexican. He did not look up from his task. The hose trembled in his hand, sending a shivering arc of water to dimple the pool's tight surface. The maid took a key from the pocket of her overall, unlocked the door of the end unit. Hazel could see her square back in the doorway, the dark snakes of hair caught in the collar of the blue denim workshirt she wore beneath her overalls. Having checked the room, the maid stepped out of it, crossed to the balcony rail and summoned the man to her with the barest movement of her head, uttering a close to imperceptible moan which Hazel picked up nonetheless as all the fine hairs on the back of her

164

neck rose in jealous antennae.

The Mexican dropped his hose which twitched across the concrete, writhed across the face of the Coke machine and reared stiffly into the sky before flopping over backwards into the pool. By this time the Mexican had reached the woman and, just before pushing her ahead of him into the room and shutting the door behind them with his thin brown foot, he raised the escaping coils of her hair, lifted them clear of her collar and kissed the nape of her neck in a gesture which bore the promise of such pleasure it caused Hazel to fall back on her bed as though shot.

'Don't,' instructed Hazel, 'please, please don't,' but she did. Water fell from her eyes, formed puddles in her ears and dribbled out again, soaking the pillow. How long could this go on, this wanting what you can't have? How deep is the ocean? How high is the sky?

FLIPPING THE SWITCH

Elizabeth Biff Ward

I

What turns me on is erotic. What is erotic turns me on.

Research shows that 95% of what passes for sex and sexual feelings occurs in the head. People have different things in their heads. Violent pornography may turn on a man for whom a stand of virgin forest, a bush cathedral, represents fifty million kitchen cupboards.

The linguistic conceit that we are 'turned on' results from the fact that we live in a society dependent on electric power. Lights get turned on. Computers. Stoves. And machines. Flip the switch. Turn me on.

What actually happens when I am turned on? I feel heat, a tingling sensation, in my loins – or groin? Or do only men have loins and groins? I feel heat, a tingling sensation, in my crotch (pronounced crutch). My crutch wants to open, be touched. When I am really turned on, I wish I was a mandrill, the multi-coloured monkey whose genitals are bright red, engorged for all the world to see. I am often amazed that so much sensation can be contained in a few flaps of skin, the tiny knob of the clitoris and a damp gooey slit under a tuft of hair. The mandrill at least shows some of what she's feeling – in truth, a good eyeful of a mandrill can be quite a turn-on.

II

I was sitting at an outdoor table in the dark.

Footsteps through the laundry stopped. I could see a shadow, huge but sharp on the concrete path in the vortex of light from the doorway. A woman leaning in the doorway, smoking. Her silhouette showed curls over her ears and at the back of her head: a curly cap. A collar winged her chin. There were tassles on her sleeves. The legs were foreshortened: a knee in blue jeans protruded.

I desired her. I was turned on: turned on by a black shadow on grey concrete. I wanted her to divine my presence, swing around into the dark, walk up to me, thrust her hand into the waistband of my trousers, pull me to my feet and push her fingers down inside my clothes and twirl them into my lips waiting.

A collar and fringes in shadow turn me on? Like this?

III

Once, in a carpark, after fucking for hours in a cave, her lover said, I want to fuck you over the bonnet of the car.

A hawk screamed and her vulva was as hot as the rocks under the spinifex.

IV

Lychee was a peach. A nutty brown shell was her only defence – when she cracked open, her glistening lychee flesh was all mine. Lychee grabbed my hand and growled, Like this! Like this!

After Lychee and my hand, her lips sucked my biceps muscle as my palm held the small of her back and we smiled in a dream while our hearts went back to walking.

Softly she said, I will put mashed strawberries and cream on you and lick it all off. As much as you like.

Lychee is definitely peachy.

V

Old lovers can be friends, dots on the horizon or people you occasionally meet. And memories. Different coloured sheets, how her breasts looked when she leaned over you, the name of her cat.

The night the woman you loved most dearly sent her clit quivering into your mouth so big and loose you thought something quite new had happened.

The one-night effort after the conference/party/dance where you wanted to scream Just do this! and that! oh please . . . and I'll never bother you again. But you didn't scream and she did something else and you knew you did the wrong thing too.

The past, memory, and the future, fantasy, can get mixed up. It is possible to be amazingly turned on by imagining perfection on a day in the future and even the person who delivers it.

She will tender to your every sexual whim most perfectly.

VI

I'm not your typical lesbian-feminist or feminist-lesbian, said Aspen. The thing is that I really enjoyed fucking with men. But fucking with women is so much better! She poured her third cup of herb tea.

Mind you, you have to find the right woman. So much of fucking is in our heads – this one doesn't like finger-fucking, that one thinks breasts are for babies and one I knew thought I was animal in bed! Well, too responsive is what she said actually. When I fuck, I want to fuck all the way. I mean, with women you don't have to wait half an hour for someone to get something up so you can be sure you have an equal number of orgasms. It's pleasure all the way. I want to have so many orgasms I lose count: I want countless orgasms to be the norm.

Amber and Moonlight giggled nervously. Frangipani looked thoughtful. What actually turns you on, Aspen?

Fucking, said Aspen. Thinking about fucking, talking about fucking, doing it. Fucking. Strong flavoured fucking. The less vanilla the better.

Amber and Moonlight giggled some more. What about love? proffered Moonlight. Aspen was looking at Frangipani who said,

Go on, Aspen.

The best thing about *Desert Hearts* was the saliva – the dribble hanging between their mouths. That's what fucking's about – saliva and sweat and juices. All the things we tidy up and put away. Fucking is over the top activity. Fucking's how you really get to know someone.

Moonlight giggled extremely nervously. Does that mean we should fuck with our friends then? She felt she'd scored a point.

Then they wouldn't be friends, they'd be lovers. Dickhead, Aspen nearly said. There's sex in every relationship. Sometimes it's more present precisely because you aren't doing it. Talking about fucking with friends is a real turn-on. The closer the friend is, the more I find myself wondering what she'd be like in bed.

Frangipani took the lid off and looked in the teapot. It's dry, she said. I agree with you, Aspen. Talking with friends can be very sexy.

Aspen smiled at her.

VII

They were friends. Special. They spent fun time together: went shopping, had picnics, lay around talking about their lovers, swapped therapies, planned holidays.

They danced well together. Not often. But if they were in the mood, they could scorch the dance floor, laughing into each other's eyes brazen. The women from other cities would watch and know that they were on together. That made them laugh more and one would put her hands into the other's armpits and they'd dance their breasts together.

Once, in a distant city, they had to share a bed after dancing the night away. Their bodies glistened with the heat and showing-off, and they lay by candlelight whispering with pleasure the stories from the party. And then they went to sleep with their bodies touching gently because they were definitely only friends.

VIII

Two women sat on a bed in a cool dark room, drenched in sweat. It was broiling heat outside. Nearing midday.

More? one smiled. They moved closer, legs splayed, and dipped some fingers into each other. They moved slightly, their mouths close and wet. After a very short while, they came together, their distended vulvas gushing liquid and sucking fingers. They clung to each other gasping, trying to laugh and moan silently so the children in the backyard would not hear.

IX

Delta was being very serious: If two women can feel that much . . . power, touch into that space . . . imagine if ten did it.

The circle gasped. Some smiled. All leaned closer.

If ten did it, she paused, looked at the ground, there'd be nowhere to go . . . Her hands came together and moved slowly upwards and apart. She was smiling. Except up. Up. Right up . . . She smiled even more. To somewhere new. We'd fly . . . or appear in another place.

Just listening like that in a discussion group, under a willow tree with no electricity anywhere near us, I was turned on. I wanted more of Delta, the poetry that came out of her mouth, her hands moving, her intent face, her huge smile. Her theory of fucking and flying.

She touched my mind: the great erogenous zone.

EROTICA

Lauren Williams

This is erotic. We kiss in the kitchen,
despite my glasses and Minnie Mouse apron.
Once our mouths find each other
they are like alkies back on a bender
. . . more, stronger, don't stop, why stop, it's too good.
We kiss like stoned musicians – endless improvisation.
Kiss, lick, slide, inside, out, tongue,
teeth connect animal fang on fang.
You suck my lip hard, you suck my tongue.
I push against you, my pelvis wants closer, to feel you.
We are stoned on each other, and that's good dope.
Your smell, sweet and smoky, warm, hair soft, mouth hot . . . oh.
We kiss, between looks into eyes that swim
in desire and wonder at us.
We make love on our feet, in the kitchen, in the afternoon,
in a house where we shouldn't be doing this,
and I am bleeding and creaming and your cock
is between my thighs as we kiss and press,
and love is a dance as we slow tango thigh to thigh,
chest to breast, tongue to tongue,
and I chase those shivers of your pleasure with my hand.
We are perfect. We are dangerous together.
We are the addict, and we are the drug.

DUBONNET ON ICE

Sue Robertson

Wouldn't it be nice, Dubonnet on ice, oh honey, it was paradise. Glance of a nought and cross, fate of feeling, isolated, a letter to a lover. The wordless space pushing the pen pauses – an uncomfortable silence of naked paper sears the eyes. I want to make love with you. I hope I see her soon. The unconscious is never enough.

Another notch on the bedpost – your knowing smile isn't 'knowing' enough, strange man. I bask within the perfection of a stranger, merely a passing flash that fails to light the eyes. Your death is never slow, your desire is never yours alone. I want your body, a temple to desecrate, a zipper catches skin – that meets – abrasive sandpaper. This isn't real, yet, here I lie, 'head in the bed' with blank face, his eyes made glassy with the sound of champagne. The sigh of a contented woman. Sandpaper, up, down, rebutt the sledgehammer called desire that splits my smile in two.

Yes it was nice, Dubonnet on ice, oh honey, it was paradise – lost. I wake early and leave.

THE DRESS

Georgia Richmond

Dee stood shivering outside the Thrift Emporium waiting impatiently for Ginny to arrive. They had arranged to meet at ten, and Ginny was late.

'Bugger this. I'm not standing out here. She'll just have to find me inside.'

Teeth chattering, she went into the warmth and made a bee-line for the books. There she threw herself into the serious business of browsing. Minutes or maybe hours later, the large pile of finds was weighing heavily in her arms.

'Have you been waiting long?' Ginny's disarming grin and hug were more than a match for the pithy comment that Dee hadn't thought up yet. 'Watcha got there?'

'Books. Can't help myself, can I? Better stop, or I won't have any money left to get this stunning outfit that you reckon I should wear to the ball.'

The two of them headed for the clothing section, watched closely by a man in a grey dustcoat. He had seen them greet each other and had decided they were worth keeping his eye on. Ginny noticed him hovering near by and nudged her friend. Grabbing Dee passionately, she made loud kissing noises and then snuggled against Dee's shoulder.

Giggling together, they began sorting through the gowns. Every few seconds they found something wild and wonderful – a bright green emerald brocade with sequin and diamante trim, a pink crêpe two piecer with seed pearls embroidered around the bodice. Eventually they reached the end of the last rack, exhausted from the hilarity of it all, but with no dress.

'Dee, you're not leaving this place without an outfit for the ball –

especially as I got up early to make sure you found one.'

'You're determined to make me tart up, aren't you? Well the only one I really fancy is the second one we looked at.'

Ginny groaned and followed her back to the start of their marathon.

'The bloody thing's not there!'

Dee flipped through the dresses again, but the object of her desire had disappeared. She looked over the racks towards the front of the shop. A woman stood at the counter with the dress slung over her arm.

'There goes my outfit, Ginny – and look at the woman who's got it. She's absolutely stunning.'

The new owner of the dress looked up. Their eyes momentarily locked in amusement and then mutual admiration, before Dee became embarrassed and looked toward Ginny for safety.

'What's up with you, eh? You're blushing.'

'I know, I can feel it. Let's go, Gin. I can cope without a dress. I think I'll just buy my books.'

'Dee, you're preoccupied again. Don't forget your coffee. It's probably getting cold now.'

Ginny was glad she had the newspaper with her. She couldn't manage to engage Dee for more than a few minutes before she shifted into another daydream. Never would have thought she'd go for the old love-at-first-sight routine. It was completely out of character for Dee. Quite the norm for Ginny, though.

They had been having a cup of coffee in this place every afternoon for the last four days, ever since Dee had seen her Mystery Woman here. That day Mystery Woman had sat by the window, talking with her two companions and casting overt glances in Dee's direction, much to her delight and Ginny's amusement.

'Ginny, that woman is gorgeous,' she said with a lustful yearn. 'I wonder who she is.'

'Dunno, but you're blushing again, kiddo.'

The trio of women had eventually scraped back their chairs. The other two loitered near the door while Mystery Woman paid the bill, again glancing directly at Dee. This time they acknowledged each other with a nod and a smile. Dee had squirmed in her seat as she watched them disappear, her pulse racing.

Days later, she was still insisting that they return each afternoon, just in case.

'Dee, come back to earth. Guess who's just about to come in. Oh, sorry, false alarm. It's not her.'

'You rat, Gin. That's not fair. I could've had a heart attack.'

They chatted briefly about the ball, deciding that they were going to put on their dancing shoes and not bother about being fancy.

The town hall was reeling from the impact of hundreds of women having a wonderful time – dancing, cuddling, talking and laughing. It was noisy and colourful and fun. At times like this, when she was part of such a huge gathering of women, Dee really felt joyful. So much positive energy around her had to rub off.

Ginny was besotted with a woman she had met a couple of hours ago, so Dee had barely seen her. They danced past each other occasionally, with Ginny winking broadly or rolling her eyes in a mute message of ecstasy.

The night was beginning to wear out for Dee when she glimpsed the dress out of the corner of her eye. She stopped dancing and stood transfixed. Just when she was in danger of being trampled to death, the music stopped. As the crush of women cleared, Dee had an uninterrupted view of the person who had become her obsession.

The dress looked superb on her.

'Dee, there you are at last. Come and meet someone from Adelaide.'

She turned reluctantly and saw her friend Jo. They were old lovers, but since Jo moved to South Australia they hadn't seen much of each other. That night the two of them had caught up with lots of news earlier in the evening, before the crowd got too big and loud.

Jo dragged her across the dance floor, clutching at her hand, suddenly sweaty as Dee realised where she was being led. They ground to a halt and Jo announced triumphantly, 'Dee, this is Chris, a friend from Adelaide. She came to live in Melbourne last month. I think you two should get to know each other.'

The two women stared at each other. Then they turned and spoke to Jo in unison.

'You're right.'

Jo smiled serenely and stepped away as the music began again.

THOSE ROSES

Lauris Edmond

Roses, the single scarlet sort,
open at the throat as if for
coolness, sprawl at the window,
you heap on my plate a pile
of potatoes, steaming and small,
smelling of mint. 'They're
basic,' you say, as we go at them
lustfully, 'they grow by the door;
you have to chase meat' – and I
notice a certain vegetable poise,
not striated, like the fibrous
deposits of a more strenuous growing,
but smooth, opaque; placid testimony
to the sufficiency of flesh.

'Of course you do have to hunt –'
I say, thinking of hopeful
burrowings in the soil, wresting
from the clutch of its black fingernails
each creamy nugget; and we agree
on that; we're a bit languid,
biting and munching more slowly
as each pale pod splits open and fills
us with amber warmth – one flesh
sturdily giving itself to another.
Those roses, too, they lean over us,
and the squat black pot gives
off its dull gleam, grinning
crookedly from the stove.

ONE WITH THE LOT

Carmel Bird

I had a pink cotton cardigan I used to wear with a linen dress. I was fourteen. The cardigan had glass buttons shaped like stars that came off a card of Lovely Lady Buttons with a picture of Ida Lupino. My mother knitted the cardigan; she was always knitting. I sewed on the buttons carefully. There were six of them, and the second from the top was out of line. I never used to do them up. 'Do up your cardigan,' my mother would say, and I would start to do it up, but when I got around the corner out of her sight I would undo it and let it flop back, flop away so that you could see the shape of nice little breasts under my linen dress. The dress was floral. It had a white background and blades of grass in clumps and bunches of primroses, and tulips that reminded me of little pink mouths. So it was really yellow and pink and green and white with a white linen collar on which my mother had sewn rick-rack braid, some green, some yellow, and some pink. It was all meant to be sweet and innocent, and it probably was if you did up your cardigan. And under the dress I had a white nylon petticoat my father gave me with a frill. The frill was embroidered with red silk hearts, and they were on the pants as well. The bra I wore was a Maidenform with a sharp point over each nipple and circles and circles of little stitches like on a breastplate. It was the points that stuck through the linen dress, and you could see them if you didn't do up the cardigan. Advertisements for Maidenform used to have a picture of a girl in a bra. The girl would be in some very unusual or inappropriate setting. So she would look like the lady from the Unicorn Tapestries except her bra would be visible, and it would say, for instance, under the picture, 'I dreamed I was a medieval maiden in my Maidenform bra.' The one I liked best was the one that said, 'I dreamed I took the bull by the horns,' but you didn't see that one very often. There was also white linen with the rick-rack on the pockets of the dress. Because it was hot I was wearing white sandals and no stockings. My legs were white and very smooth because I had just shaved them with a little green Milady razor, and I had sandpapered them with a Silkymit. Under my arms I just did with the razor, and I plucked my eyebrows. I knew a girl who used to pluck the hairs on her arms. My lipstick was pale pink to match the cardigan and very thick. There was a place in George Street called the Rainbow where girls from school were not allowed to go. It was out of bounds because you met boys there and had ice-cream sundaes and it smelt of sour milk and Californian Poppy Oil. I was meeting Geoffrey Reynolds in the Rainbow and we had enough money between us to have the special which was One with the Lot. My linen dress had a full circle skirt that my mother had gone to a lot of trouble over. Geoffrey was sixteen. Once I made it up in my diary that he kissed me, and my mother read it, and I wasn't supposed to see him. It seemed pointless to explain I was making the diary up; not only pointless but embarrassing, and probably worse. There was a person I had really kissed the time I wrote it up as Geoffrey. This was Harvey Chappell, and he was brainy and couldn't dance and only said about three things all night. Once he said he was reading a book about people who were so poor they had to eat baby crocodiles. I think it was in New Guinea or somewhere. Harvey's mother had the most awful way of cutting up oranges. She would get the orange on the vegetable board and cut it in half like through the equator. Then she would put the halves cut-side down on the board and cut really thin slices. Then she scraped the board into the sink and put the slices on a pink saucer. She would sit down at the kitchen table and pull the flesh of the orange off the slices with her teeth. She had very terrible false teeth. And she would wipe her mouth with her apron and tip the slices of orange peel into a sheet of newspaper to wrap up for the garbage. Bits of orange stayed stuck in her teeth. Harvey was nice really, but he trod on my foot. So I met Geoffrey at the Rainbow, and we ordered spiders as well as One with the Lot, which meant two kinds of ice-cream and strawberry syrup and fruit and cream and nuts and chocolate shavings and a glacé cherry and wafers and two spoons in a huge glass dish like a boat. I was wearing vanilla as perfume and my Eastern Star ring. Geoffrey and I were sitting tight up against each other in the corner where people in the street couldn't see us. I took off my cardigan because I was hot and got syrup down the front of my dress just a little bit. I was thinking about what I wrote in the diary and wishing it was true and wondering how it would be if I said anything about it as a sort of joke somehow. Then he put his arm right around me, and I felt really quite uncomfortable and wanted to run. The table had a grey and white marble top. I just kept slowly digging my spoon into the ice-cream and nuts and syrup and pushing it against the side of the dish and then eating. It would melt in my mouth and slide down easily, but the taste was very sickly, and I had to chew the nuts. For some reason it was embarrassing sitting there with Geoffrey's arm around me, saying nothing, and chewing and swallowing. I had eaten off my lipstick by then. The main reason the Rainbow was out of bounds was because you would kiss and cuddle in there and later on there would be passionate scenes in parked cars and on verandahs. The sort of scenes I would never actually put in my diary whether I was making it up or not. This was the first time I had ever been to the Rainbow and Geoffrey was kissing my hair and so I swallowed a big blob of ice-cream and turned around so we could kiss on the lips. And we did. It was completely different from Harvey because Geoffrey kind of pushed his tongue between my teeth, and I was surprised at first but I liked it slipping in and out like a lizard. Afterwards we didn't finish the sundae, and I left my cardigan on the seat. I meant to go back for it, but I never did.

MY BLUESTONE RING

Edith Speers

it's there in all the pictures
of that time
hand on a purple velour hip
big silver ring a real knuckleduster
left hand middle finger
and the big blue stone like a robin's egg
to my eye the centre of the picture
whatever smiles and limbs
pose around it

it weighed a lot
it was never forgotten on my finger
I was always aware
and liked the way it anchored my hand
or maybe ballast is a better word
something anyway that impeded
that dignified
the kneading of bread the grip of a hoe
the otherwise aimless gesture

it was my wedding ring I decided
the one I never wanted to own
not a real diamond and a signed licence
in the kitchen drawer
sort of thing
but my secret pact sky blue and silver
that this was my one and only
my once in a lifetime husband
even if he didn't know it

then when things were getting bad
I took a trip on my own
first time in four years I'd even been off
the farm so no wonder
I was scared
but I had a pair of red highheel leather boots
and bought two new pairs of jeans
and a silk shirt
and spent my money on booze and movies

it was great
my friends liked me how I was
and my face remembered
how to forget to compose itself into a shape
forever asking forgiveness forever
puzzled forever
tight wrinkled between the brows
except on social occasions
or at work

and there was a red-haired man
two of them actually brothers
friends of my girlfriend I was staying with
and her husband
but the one without a woman
was the bigger of the two going to beerbelly big
but not yet
not for a year or two yet and he was tall
and I knew he liked me

it was Sunday night
and I was catching a plane the next Saturday morning
I had the ticket
and the one letter in two months my man had sent me
a poem and two hundred dollars but he was too late
I lay in bed past eleven pm
thinking and thinking about that red-haired man
there was no time left
and I asked myself do you want him

and I answered yes I want him
so I got out of bed
and got dressed

and left a note for my friend on the fridge door
that said gone prowling
see you whenever
and when I got outside I pulled on my boots
closed the door softly and tiptoed away from the house
because I didn't want to answer any questions

it was bright outside
because this was the city with street lights
the pavement was wet and clicked
under my boot heels
and on the grass there were still icy frozen foam
patches of snow that glittered
I had grown up in this city and as I walked quickly
but not too quickly to my lover's place
I slid my ring off and into my pocket

the light was on
he was sitting up drinking beer with his brother
talking about their boat
and I said I just felt like visiting
which I'd done before but at noon not midnight
the brother was drunk but not so drunk
he couldn't see straight
and bless him
cleared out while he was still able

we talked the red-haired man and me
we sat at the kitchen table
for way too long
until I began to wonder if I shouldn't take the hint
and get going
except I was so certain of him maybe it was me
who was holding back
so when we finally sat on the sofa I kissed his ear
and he understood me

he had a water bed
the first I've ever slept in but he was so heavy on top of me
my spine could feel the boards underneath
and every move
seemed to make a tidal wave
but it wasn't until a few days later

I found all that out
because that first night he couldn't stay hard
no matter what we did we got nowhere

the next day we went on a ferry boat
and stayed at a hotel
he asked for a room with a view of the ocean
and as soon as we got inside
he took my hand and we lay on the bed but it was bad as ever
he lay back as white as a beached whale
so fine a skin
you see on a red-haired man then I said
close your eyes and go to sleep

as I straddled him
relax I said and just go to sleep
as I kissed his nipples so tiny for such a big man
but sensitive as a woman's they stood up
and he grew harder the more
I bit and licked
but once he tried to move and I spoke in anger lie still
because moving made him soften so then he gave in
and it worked and I was glad to get him inside me

he was not a big man
but I was glad of him and held him tight
he kept his eyes closed
and we kissed while I moved for both of us until he groaned
and cried out such a cry I asked
are you all right
he was all right
he called it my magic and after that
we got along fine together

we didn't even have every night
my friend said it was exciting she'd never seen him
with a woman before
in the five years she'd known him
he scared his brother the way he drove back late on Friday
and early on Saturday morning I got dressed
kissed the palm of his hand said I love you
and dropped tears
into his cupped hand goodbye goodbye always sounds phony

I had to go back
I was hungover and sick and some stupid Pom
in the seat behind me
kept bumping the back of my seat his girlfriend was screechy
and I got so mad
at his long legs pointy shoes
shoving around underneath me I tipped out the dregs
of my salad coleslaw wet with dressing all over his feet
in plain view and bugger them all

and on the other side waiting
was the man I'd lived with for six years
things just got worse
but so slowly
it was one year later exactly
that I got out of his bed for the last time it's funny
he'd bought a water bed
I haven't worn the ring since then but I still turn
in the street to look at a red-haired man

BEYOND THIS MORNING

Jenny Boult

After forty-five minutes the man in seat 27 takes off his artificial leg. It is pink and made of plastic and wears a grey and red tartan sock and a highly polished brown lace-up shoe. The leg is hairless and has a leather strap near the top. The strap is reflected in the heel of the shoe. The man rests his stump on the leg and leans down to take off the shoe he is wearing on his good leg. He stretches his toes on the cool of the air conditioning that blows around his ankle.

When the ticket men come, he pretends to be asleep and snores erratically. The taller of the two looks at him and then moves on without waking him. The railway workers on the line outside peer in through the windows and watch the passengers curiously. They all look similar in the brown seats, and they soon stop and lean back on their shovels.

I roll along the aisle to the door marked Ladies. The toilet is a bowl with a hole, and the wind blows up on my cunt. I think about the way you suck me off and wonder how long it will take for the fullness inside me to go away. I see you in the half-light of memory and catch my breath.

The man in seat 27 looks at me and smiles slightly as though he is reading my thoughts, and he eases his stump against the separated calf and slides into the shallow sleep of the train see-sawing along the tracks.

The man with one leg has a wife with an Oroton cigarette case. She has a small mouth that curves down at the corners, and she looks at him with a scathing glance, which he accepts as he shuffles in his seat.

My eyes are pricking. I tell myself it is only the cigarette smoke and remember that I told myself 'no tears'. The communication cord looks exotic and invites a sharp pull, but I do not pull it. The poem you wrote me and *The Fat Man in History* fall out of the luggage rack onto the sleeping children in the seat in front. They do not wake up. And then a flurry of papers falls on me. The one-legged man's wife, who is wearing blue, helps me pick up the typed pages. She has a short story in her hand and is reluctant to give it to me. She asks me if I am a writer and I tell her 'of sorts'. She looks at the story in her hand, I tell her she can read it if she likes, but she nods at the Women's Weekly romance on her seat and then squints at me. She gives me the story, thrusting at me as though it is hot in her hand. I take it from her and re-arrange the manila folders and the papers in the plastic bag and replace it all in the luggage rack.

I don't mind if your car rattles and shakes, or that your bed is noisy and creaks, or that you are ten years older than me and own property.

The man has put his leg back on. The place where the two sections join in is lumpy and thick.

The Italians further down the carriage are talking, but I cannot understand them. The children look a little like chickens, and I remember the film we saw, and then I see that they are eating bread and chocolate. My cunt slowly begins to contract until it is so tight even your little finger could not squeeze in there.

I am whispering into a sheet of old computer paper with a black plastic biro. I did not take a shower this morning, it was deliberate. I face the window and slide my hand down into my pants and it is wet and satiny and now my fingers smell of you. And I want to wank somewhere, quietly, with that smell, but the toilet is ugly and the washroom is bare and overbright. I want to shelter somewhere in a dark corner with a faint light that is red and pulses slightly.

I lean against the washroom sink, which is cold against my arse and slip my fingers down. There is a big mirror on the back of the door, and my thighs tremble and it is good.

The man across the aisle has taken his leg off again, and I have an uncontrollable urge to fill it with Coca-Cola and watch the brown bubbles fizz over the top, and I am glad I am a woman.

The man with one leg is sitting with his friend. His wife is sitting with the other man's wife, and all four are smoking and drinking beer. The woman attempts elegance with the silvery cigarette case but fails. Her fingers are gnarled with arthritis, and her husband is filling his calf with empty beer cans so that they do not roll about on the floor.

The conductor walks down the aisle carrying a large yellow plastic bag and asks if anyone has any rubbish. The man empties his leg into the bag and a man in a brown suit scowls at him. I am so busy watching them that I do not realise that my ashtray is full until he has gone. I ash my cigarette on the floor and try to look as though it is the correct thing to do. And I do it so much more elegantly than the woman with the arthritic fingers and a glittering cigarette case. She looks at me and I beam at her, but she does not meet my eyes and turns away back to her friend and her tinny. My face is frozen in a tetanoid grin, which she cannot handle at all.

The train crawls over a metal bridge with high sides. There are several crucified bodies hanging from the cross beams, but I do not know why. The gum trees lining the track are weeping in the sunlight and are full of huge butterflies laying eggs.

The man with the stump drops another can into his leg shell and pokes at his wife through the gap in the seats and looks at her fiercely. She gets up and takes her purse from her handbag and starts to walk towards the buffet car. She leans at me and asks me what I am writing. I tell her that it is a science fiction epic. She does not believe me. I can tell.

I remember the strange bug that walked up my arm in your kitchen. I watched it for a while and then killed it.

THE STORM

Robyn Rowland

'*so you refuse and then you discover that your
house is haunted by the ghost of a leopard.*'

Jeanette Winterson, *The Passion*

I dream of your want,
shock awake to it
throbbing the air
breaking white fire
stretched bare
striating the sky.

So fierce
a lather of light to write by.
Thunder of your need crackling,
desire rockets over the night
beating up winds to
pummel the silky oak
grevillea robusta,
throwing off rain wanton, in a
shaggy shaking from the hidden den.

Noise and flash detonate synchronous
rocking foundations.
I feel you here
so far across the oceans
your scent buried deep.
You should not have come so far
on such a night.

You should not have called all this up
dynamitic and raging.

I rise naked in the dark tremble.
You blaze clapping behind me
firm palms warm on the shoulders
breath sweet at the nape,
turning me, you take my cool wrist
laying your burning cheek against it
sliding your tongue up long inside my arm
then say, 'choose;
let me love you.'

'But passion is spent, past,
frightening thrill of it no longer seduces.'
Yet you tempt, still,
with your night-wild yearning,
stirring the pink softness of fig flesh,
membranes' fragile betrayal.

Anyway,
it's only a storm.

The Integration of Creativity and Sexuality

Jesse Kate Blackadder

Make the bread do the dishes feed the cats go to the shop run my hand over your soft hard stomach write the script prepare the submission try to get money try not to get caught bite the soft part in your instep throw out the dead flowers start the novel draw a storyboard make the bed smell your body on the sheets pay the bill post the letter arrive in time stay in bed melt melt ring the lawyer borrow money steal money ask for a favour pull your breast in my mouth this is not a poem find a place to insert punctuation find the place where my fingers fit your legs fit my mouth fits but then it runs over the side and escapes turn on the light turn off the light do you like to do it in the dark type up the next draft get the washing machine fixed buy tampons wash the sheets sometime this month try to find another crooked doctor another dole form doctored this is good for your health relax your body clear the table try to remember the idea from yesterday pull out the dictionary answer the phone look up the deadline too late your mouth on mine merging the phone ringing change the lightglobe meditate feed the cats clean the window get a view find a perspective find that spot at the base of your spine look up this week's stars find just the right way find your cunt flowing till the room fills up find me drowning find you gasping for breath find the typewriter under the stairs find my fingers waiting inside you find the words find the time drop my head down there find your thigh find the pulse that beats elusive remember to breathe my fingers on the keys going in further and further my mouth on your breast yes my hands running away yes yes my tongue your lips drowning reaching further and deeper the pulse beat against my fingertip your hand the colours the words slithering out on sweat streams before spoken disappearing useless the typewriter melts slowly as the temperature rises the electric blanket catches on fire my teeth sink into the fleshy part of your thumb the lightglobe overloads and blows out the cats eat each other one finger at a time then two then three your cunt expands effortlessly my hand my arm my shoulder still reaching my face my tongue my body slithers inside my uterus heaves you come slowly out on the bed in a pool of mucus born you clamber on my stomach everything fills your limbs sprawl tiny across my belly you breathe crying my breast aching our sweat merges breathing merges one last gasp for air the skin parts the words part I fall into your mouth the colours the phone explodes you scream I pant you go deeper I want the window cracks your tongue on mine the paper absorbs moisture I choke turns to mush I slide underneath you turns to liquid the bed is mixed chopped whirled blended puréed we cease to exist.

TALKING ABOUT SEX

Jenny Pausacker

'Mm, yes, like that.'

'So I'd be sitting at my desk, reading through all this heavy semiotic theory, and suddenly I'd have to go and masturbate. It really turned me on.'

'I like breasts. Big breasts.'

'Me too.'

'We slept in the same room, but with her parents on the other side of the wall we didn't feel like doing anything. Then on Sunday we went for a walk along the beach. A few metres out in the sea, there was this big rock. We waded over to it and on the far side we found this shelf, just big enough to fit both of us . . .'

'. . . right by the side of the track, and we were just zipping our jeans again when three families came marching along, one after the other . . .'

'So we were fucking away, having a wonderful time, when suddenly Carmel yells, 'Twenty.' She'd been counting my orgasms and she was so impressed that she ran out to the kitchen and opened a bottle of champagne. We sat on the end of Lou and Jane's bed and drank toasts together.'

'How would you feel if – if I touched myself and you just watched? Held me.'

'Sal found an old pair of silk bloomers at the Op shop – very soft, very sensual and *very* wide in the leg. She put them on, and I slid my hand up slowly, inch by inch, while she pretended not to notice.'

'It was like in *The Never-ending Story* where Artreyu rides the luck-dragon, plunging up and down.'

'There's Martina. See the way her left arm's bigger than her right arm. Those tennis-playing muscles.'

'I used to listen to you and Marie from across the hall, masturbate sometimes.'

'Do you? Do you? Oh, I *couldn't*.'

'So there were all these heavy New York dykes in their leathers, looking cooler than anything I'd ever seen in my life. What did we do? Well, we had one quick drink and then left, what else?'

'Once to wake myself up in the morning, then at work in the toilets, sometimes twice a day, and at night, of course, so I could go to sleep.'

'I just love hairy legs.'

'On the couch.'

'In the car.'

'In the hallway.'

'When my mother was in the top bunk.'

'More. Please.'

'It was pretty late by the time we'd finished talking, so she just hopped into the single bed with me. We snuggled up and then, well, we were fucking. When I opened my eyes next morning, the other woman who was sharing the room with us went scooting off to the bathroom, carrying all her clothes. I think we must have freaked her out, which was pretty funny, 'cos she worked as a sex therapist.'

'I used to imagine I was this Scottish girl, Jane McDonald, who was intrepid, rescuing Bonnie Prince Charlie, and things like that. Then I hit puberty, and poor Jane started to get into all these masochistic scenes with guys.'

'You did? Good on you. And what did she say?'

'She's a fabulous kisser.'

'Both of us had been celibate for a while, and we'd started to make a big production out of the times when we went out together, finding interesting restaurants and coffee shops, and that. It was my turn, and I had it all worked out – curry, video games, an ice-cream sundae and then, as we were getting into the car, I said, "There's another pleasant thing we could do."'

'So she came home one day, raving about this terrific new graffiti – "Lesbianism, a good lick." It sounded kind of strange to me, and then later I was driving around and I saw it – "Lesbianism, a nice slip of the tongue."'

'Do you do that too? I thought I was the only person.'

'We told them that we'd never even tried penetration, because it was male-defined, and they laughed for ages.'

'Fruit, for example – kiwi fruit were the best. And once Kay had a bottle of Tia Maria, so she poured it over me and licked it off. The sheets got a bit sticky, but.'

Four fingers inside her. Just from kissing my ear. KY jelly. So that our clitorises actually touch – it's hard to find the right angle. What *is* tribadism? Against her breast. At the same time, of course. We tried it once, but basically that was enough.

'Slower.'

'Faster.'

'Oh yes.'

'I like sex.'

'I like cuddles best.'

'I need sex.'

'I like talking about sex.'

THE DIARY OF EMBRACES

Antonia Bruns

He embraces me, I am lying naked.
My belly and hips are Delta.

He embraces me in the car. He holds me from the waist up.
He bites my lip. I remember this much later.

I embrace him. He says I am holding him like a soft toy,
an egg inside.

We embrace, we are joined at head and heart. He says he feels
great tenderness.

We embrace in water. I sit in his lap like a mermaid.

We embrace. I am a playboy bunny. My legs are very long.
My waist is very small.

We embrace beneath white sheets and hold each other as buds.

We embrace and she is my twin. My head is at her feet.

We embrace and she feels like a ripe pear.

He embraces me as a man who cannot forget his authority.

We embrace and release.

I embrace a sailor.

We embrace and my hair comb scrapes his cheek.

We embrace and she is my heart.

We do not embrace, and I cannot approach for fear of
imposing.

We cannot embrace because I will fall in love.

He stabs me with his embrace.
We hide in our embrace.
We are covered in blood, we are covered in blood.

I embrace myself.

We embrace for years.

NOTES ON CONTRIBUTORS

JACQUELINE BARRETT was born in Newcastle in 1944. She has worked as a teacher and a librarian, and is now a quiltmaker living in Leura in the Blue Mountains. Her poetry has been published in *Womanspeak, Refractory Girl* and *New Poetry* magazines, and in the anthology *Up From Below: Poems of the 1980s* (Redress, 1987). She is married (and once divorced) and has three children.

JOAN BIRCHALL emigrated from England in 1953. She has won a number of literary awards for short story writing. Her work has been published in England and Australia and broadcast by the BBC, ABC and Radio Adelaide 5UV. She has had articles published in newspapers and national magazines.

CARMEL BIRD was born in Tasmania in 1940. She has published *Births, Deaths and Marriages* (Power Press, 1983), *Cherry Ripe* (Power Press, 1985), *The Woodpecker Toy Fact* (McPhee Gribble, 1987), *Dear Writer* (McPhee Gribble, 1988), and *Woodpecker Point* (New Directions, 1988).

JESSE KATE BLACKADDER was born in Sydney in 1964. A Gemini with Pisces rising, she graduated from NSW Institute of Technology with a BA in Communications, majoring in film and writing. She is currently establishing a film production company, working on a book about sexuality, and planning to learn the saxaphone.

JENNY BOULT writes poetry, drama and fiction from her home in suburban Adelaide. She has been widely anthologised and has had seven books published to date. Most recently *About Auntie Rose* (Omnibus/Puffin, 1988), which is a collection of poetry for children.

DIANE BROWN was born in Unley, South Australia. She was a force behind the formation of the Association of Country and City Writers (SA). She is an editorial collective member of *Angry Women* anthology (Hale and Iremonger, 1989) and the founder and administrator of Tantrum Press. She is currently studying Arts Administration and lives in Adelaide.

ANTONIA BRUNS was born in Melbourne in 1957. She has co-edited two Fringe Network anthologies, *Exiles in Paradise/ Network* (1983) and *Soft Lounges* (1984). Her work has been published by various small presses. An independent filmmaker, she has made 'Metaphors' (1985) and 'Campanile' (1986). She is currently studying architecture and film for an MArch, as well as co-producing and writing a series of documentaries on contemporary Australian architecture.

CORNELIA CARMAN was born in the USA in 1935. She is now an expatriate, living in country Victoria.

DAWN COHEN was born in 1957. She is a writer, performer and psychotherapist. She has previously had work published in *Words from the Same Heart* (Hale and Iremonger, 1988) and *Up From Below: Poems of the 1980s* (Redress Press, 1987).

ANNA COUANI lives in Sydney where she works as an art teacher. She is a small press publisher and belongs to the No Regrets Women Writers Group. Her published works include *Italy and the Train* (Sea Cruise, 1986) and *Were All Women Sex-Mad* (Rigmarole, 1982). Her fourth book, *The Harbour Breathes* is a collaboration with visual artist, Peter Lyssiotis. Her work is available from Sea Cruise Books, 28 Queen Street, Glebe, Sydney.

SARA DOWSE was born in Chicago, USA. She has published *West Block* (Penguin, 1983) and *Silver City* (Penguin, 1984) and contributed to *Canberra Tales* (Penguin, 1988). She lives in Canberra.

LAURIS EDMOND was born in Hawkes Bay, New Zealand in

1924. She has published nine books of poetry, most recently *Summer near the Arctic Circle* (1988), one novel, several plays for radio and one stage play. She lives in Wellington, New Zealand, and is currently working on an autobiography, the first volume of which is *Hot October* (1989).

MARIAN ELDRIDGE was born in Victoria in 1936. She is now writing full-time in Canberra. She has published *Walking the Dog and Other Stories* (UQP, 1984), *The Woman at the Window* (UQP, 1989) and she is a contributor to *Canberra Tales* (Penguin, 1988).

KATHLEEN MARY FALLON was born in Monto, Queensland in 1951. She grew up in Brisbane and now lives and works in Sydney. She is published in various anthologies and magazines. Her published books are *Implosion, Explosion* (1980), *Sexuality of Illusion* (1981), and more recently *Working Hot* (Sybylla Press, 1989). Her play, 'Spill' was performed in Sydney in 1987.

BEVERLEY FARMER was born in Melbourne in 1941. She has published *Alone* (Sisters Publishing, 1980), *Milk* (McPhee Gribble/Penguin, 1983) and *Home Time* (McPhee Gribble/Penguin, 1985). She lives in Point Lonsdale.

JOANNE FINKELSTEIN was born in Melbourne in 1950. She has published *Dining Out: A Sociology of Modern Manners* (Polity, 1989). Currently she is a lecturer in the Department of Anthropology and Sociology, Monash University, Victoria.

JILL GOLDEN was born in Sydney in 1941. She has published *Jess* (Tantrum Press, 1987) and lives and works in Adelaide.

MARION HALLIGAN was born in Newcastle. She has published a novel, *Self Possession* (UQP, 1987), two collections of short stories, *The Living Hothouse* (UQP, 1988), and *The Hanged Man in the Garden* (Penguin, 1989); and is one of the seven writers of *Canberra Tales* (Penguin, 1988).

BARBARA HANRAHAN was born in Adelaide in 1939. Since her first book, *The Scent of Eucalyptus* (Chatto and Windus, 1973) she has published nine other novels and a collection of short stories *Dream People* (Grafton, 1987). A printmaker, as well as a writer, her work is represented in the Australian National Gallery, state and regional galleries. After many years in London, she now lives in Adelaide.

GILLIAN HANSCOMBE was born in Melbourne in 1945. She has published *Hecate's Charms* (Khasmik Press, 1976); *Between Friends* (Alyson Publications, Boston, 1982; Sheba, London, 1983; forthcoming The Women's Press, London, 1990); *The Art of Life: Dorothy Richardson and the development of feminist consciousness* (Peter Owen, London, 1982; Ohio University Press, 1983); *Flesh and Paper*, co-authored with Suniti Namjoshi (Ragweed Press, Canada, 1986; Jezebel Tapes and Books, Seaton, UK, 1986); and *Writing for Their Lives: The Modernist Women, 1910–1949*, co-authored with Virginia L. Smyers (The Women's Press, London, 1987; Northeastern University Press, Boston, 1988). She lives in the UK.

SUSAN HAWTHORNE was born in 1951. She works as an editor and reviewer. Her short stories, poems, articles and reviews have been published in magazines and books in Australia and overseas. She is the editor of *Difference: Writings by Women* (Brooks Waterloo, 1985).

HELEN HODGMAN was born in Aberdeen, Scotland in 1945. She has published *Blue Skies* (Penguin, 1975) and *Jack and Jill* (Penguin, 1978) which won the Somerset Maugham Award (a single volume edition has been reprinted by Virago, 1989). *Broken Words* (Penguin, 1988) is her third novel. After living overseas for many years, she now lives in Sydney and is writing for film and television.

DOROTHY HORSFIELD was born in Newcastle, NSW. She is a journalist and a writer, and has published short stories and articles in literary magazines and newspapers, and a book *Canberra Tales* (Penguin, 1988) with six other women. She lives in Canberra.

STEPHANIE JOHNSON was born in 1961 in Auckland, New Zealand. She has published poetry, *The Bleeding Ballerina* (Hard Echo Press, NZ), and short stories, *The Glass Whittler* (The New Women's Press, NZ, 1988; Penguin, 1989). She also writes stage and screen plays. She is now living in Sydney.

ROSEMARY JONES was born in Adelaide, South Australia, in

1954. She has had stories published in magazines such as *Australian Short Stories* and in anthologies, including *Room to Move* (Redress Press/Allen and Unwin, 1985) and *Unsettled Areas* (Wakefield Press, 1986). She has taught in high schools for the past twelve years and is now living in a dug out in Cooper Pedy and teaching English.

DONNA McSKIMMING was born in Brisbane in 1957. She has published a book of poetry, *Beware the Bouganvillea* (Friendly Street Poets, 1986). She lives in Adelaide.

JANE MEREDITH was born in 1964. A Gemini, she is currently living/writing in the Dandenongs outside Melbourne and analysing the politics of love and power.

FINOLA MOORHEAD was born in Melbourne in 1947. A writer in a sweatshirt she has published in various literary magazines and anthologies since 1973 and writes for theatre now and then. Her books include a novel, *Remember the Tarantella* (Primavera, 1987); short prose, *Quilt* (Sybylla, 1985); and a personal manifesto, *A Handwritten Modern Classic* (Post Neo, 1985). She continues to write and has been assisted by the Literature Board of the Australia Council in 1988 and 1989.

KAYE MOSELEY was born in Melbourne in 1952. She works as a teacher of Art and English.

MERRILEE MOSS was born in Canberra in 1950. She is a playwright and has published short stories, teenage fiction, critical articles and reviews. She lives in Melbourne.

HELEN PAUSACKER was born in Melbourne in 1954. She now works as a secretary and has been involved with the mixed gay movement for the last ten years.

JENNY PAUSACKER works as a freelance writer. Her novel for teenagers, *What Are Ya?*, which explores the issue of choice and sexuality, won the Angus and Robertson Junior Writers Fellowship in 1985.

GEORGIA RICHMOND was born in Warrnambool, Victoria in 1946. She survived boarding school, child-rearing and living in a country town. She now lives and works in Melbourne.

SUE ROBERTSON lives in Brisbane and writes short fiction.

ROBYN ROWLAND was born in Sydney in 1952. She lived mostly on the south coast of New South Wales until her twenties, when she moved to New Zealand for three years. She has published poetry, *Filigree in Blood* (Longman Cheshire, 1982) and *Perverse Serenity* (Heinemann, forthcoming 1990), and feminist theory, *Woman Herself* (Oxford, 1988). She has been widely published in Australia and internationally and is currently a Senior Lecturer in Women's Studies, Deakin University, Victoria.

SANDRA SHOTLANDER was born in Melbourne in 1941. She is a playwright, performer, founder/director of several theatre companies (The Plantagenets and Mime and Mumbles). She also writes short stories. Her published plays include *Framework* (Yackandandah, 1983) *Blind Salomé* (Yackandandah, 1985); *Collected Plays* (Wild Iris Press, Winter Park, USA, 1988). Her unpublished plays are 'Full Circle', 'Angels of Power' and a radio play, 'Just One More Thing'.

EDITH SPEERS was born in Canada in 1949. She arrived in Australia in 1974. She has been published in various literary magazines here and overseas. She trained as a biochemist and now lives on a farm in southern Tasmania. She has published a book of poetry, *By Way of a Vessel* (Twelvetrees Publishing Co., 1986).

LEONE SPERLING was born in Sydney in 1937. She has published *Coins for the Ferryman* (Pan Books, 1981) and *Mother's Day* (Redress Press/Wild and Woolley, 1984). Several short stories have been published in newspapers and anthologies. She lives in Sydney and teaches English at North Sydney College of TAFE.

JENNIFER STRAUSS was born in Heywood, Victoria in 1933. She has published *Children and Other Strangers* (Nelson, 1975), *Winter Driving* (Sisters Publishing, 1981), and *Labour Ward* (Pariah, 1988). She is currently a lecturer in the Department of English, Monash University, Victoria.

ANIA WALWICZ was born in Poland in 1951. She has published

Writing (Rigmarole Books, 1982; reprinted by Angus and Robertson, 1989) and *Boat* (Angus and Robertson, 1989).

ELIZABETH BIFF WARD was born in Sydney in 1942. She has published *Father-Daughter Rape* (The Women's Press, 1984). She works as a writer and also as a trainer in the human resource area, specialising in equal opportunity issues. She lives in Adelaide.

TERRY WHITEBEACH is forty-one years old, and presently living in Hobart with two of her three teenage children. She is a writer and adult education tutor. With the assistance of a grant from the Aboriginal Arts Board, she is writing a book about Tasmanian Aboriginal women. She has ideologically unsound views on most things, including sex.

LAUREN WILLIAMS was born in Melbourne in 1958. She has edited *Big Bang*, an independent literary magazine, and is a performance poet, singer and rapper.

ACKNOWLEDGEMENTS

For permission to reprint the works in this anthology, acknowledgement is made to the following:

Jacqueline Barrett: 'Sometimes When We Fuck', previously published in *Up From Below: Poems of the 1980s*, (1987), Women's Redress Press Inc., Sydney, to the author.

Joan Birchall: 'Seven for a Secret Never to be Told', to the author.

Carmel Bird: 'One with the Lot', previously published in *Woodpecker Point* (1988), New Directions, N.Y.; and in *Fine Line*, No. 4, 1988, to the author.

Jesse Kate Blackadder: 'A Fantasy' and 'The Integration of Creativity and Sexuality', to the author.

Jenny Boult: 'Beyond This Morning', previously published in *"i" is a versatile character*, (1986), WAV Publications, Adelaide, to the author.

Diane Brown: 'Now That's Erotic', to the author.

Antonia Bruns: 'The Diary of Embraces', previously published in slightly different versions in *Soft Lounges: The 2nd Fringe Anthology* (1984), Fringe Network, Melbourne; and in *Telling Ways: Australian Women's Experimental Writing*, (1988) Australian Feminist Studies Publications, Adelaide, to the author.

Cornelia Carman: 'The Miracle Healer', to the author.

Dawn Cohen: 'Lesbian Heaven', previously published in *Up From Below: Poems of the 1980s*, (1987), Women's Redress Press Inc., Sydney, to the author.

Anna Couani: 'The Map of the World', previously published in *The Train/Leaving Queensland* by Anna Couani/Barbara Brooks (1983), Sea Cruise Books, Sydney; and *Italy and The Train* (1985), Rigmarole Books, Melbourne; and *The Penguin Book of Australian Women Poets* (1986), Penguin, Ringwood, to the author.

Sara Dowse: 'Fugue on Forty', previously published in *Island Magazine*, No. 27, 1986, to the author.

Lauris Edmond: 'Those Roses', previously published in *Meanjin*, Vol. 39, No. 2, 1980, to the author.

Marian Eldridge: 'A Love Story', previously published in *Kunapipi,* Vol. VIII, No. 1, 1986; and in *The Woman at the Window*, (1989), UQP, Brisbane, to the author and to UQP.

Mary Fallon: 'The Sexuality of Illusion', extract from *The Sexuality of Illusion*, Working Hot, Sydney, 1981, to the author.

Beverley Farmer: 'Figs', to the author.

Joanne Finkelstein: 'Sex in the Modern State', to the author.

Jill Golden: 'Callistemon', previously published in *Masks*, (1988), Association of Country and City Writers, Adelaide, to the author.

Marion Halligan: 'Paternity Suit', previously published in *Southerly*, Vol. 4, 1984; 'Use More Hooks', previously published in *Island Magazine*, No. 18/19, 1984; both were published in *The Hanged Man in the Garden* (1989), Penguin, Ringwood, to the author and to Penguin.

Barbara Hanrahan: 'Butterfly', to the author.

Gillian Hanscombe: 'Fragment', previously published in *Flesh and Paper*, (1986) by Gillian Hanscombe and Suniti Namjoshi, Jezebel Tapes and Books, UK; and in *A Double Colonization: Colonial and Post-Colonial Women's Writing*, (1986), Dangaroo Press, Mundelstrup, Denmark, to the author.

Susan Hawthorne: 'Erotica Alphabetica' to the author; 'Two Photographs' previously published in *On the Off Beat*, No. 2, 1987, to the author.

Helen Hodgman: 'How High is the Sky', extract (slightly different version) from *Broken Words* (1988), Penguin Books, Ringwood, to the author.

Dorothy Horsfield: 'Keeping Fit', previously published in *Canberra Tales*, (1988) Penguin, Ringwood, to the author.

Stephanie Johnson: 'The Invisible Hand' and 'Poking the Peevish

Gutter', previously published in *The Glass Whittler* (1988), New Women's Press, Auckland and (1989) Penguin Books, Ringwood, to the author.

Rosemary Jones: 'Magill Road', previously published in *Australian Short Stories*, No. 15, 1986; 'The Woman in the Moon' broadcast on 'Writers' Radio' 5UV, 1987, to the author.

Donna McSkimming: 'Gardenia' previously published in *No. 10 Friendly Street Poetry Reader*, (1986) Friendly Street Poets, Adelaide; 'Ululation for a Red-headed Woman', previously published in *Up From Below: Poems of the 1980s* (1987) Women's Redress Press Inc., Sydney, to the author.

Jane Meredith: 'Edges', to the author.

Finola Moorhead: 'The Last Pages of Ulysses', previously published in *H/ear 7, Being Here* (Part 1), ES/43, Summer 84/84, TMCON 10, to the author.

Kaye Moseley: 'Muriel and the Tiger', broadcast as a three-voice piece on 'Give Men-a-Pause', 3RRR, 1980, to the author.

Merrilee Moss: 'Erotic as Anything', previously published in *Outrage*, No. 3, June, 1983, to the author.

Helen Pausacker: 'Red as a Beetroot', to the author.

Jenny Pausacker: 'Resurrection of the Body' and 'Talking About Sex', to the author.

Georgia Richmond: 'The Dress', to the author.

Sue Robertson: 'Dubonnet on Ice'.

Robyn Rowland: 'The Storm', to the author.

Sandra Shotlander: 'Telephone Conversation in a Common Language', to the author.

Edith Speers: 'Why I Like Men', previously published in *The Penguin Book of Australian Women Poets* (1986) Penguin, Ringwood, to the author; 'My Bluestone Ring', to the author.

Leone Sperling; 'The Man with the Magic Phallus', extract from *Coins for the Ferryman* (1981), Pan Books, Sydney, to the author.

Jennifer Strauss: 'Loving Parents', previously published in *Children and Other Strangers* (1975) Thomas Nelson, Melbourne; and in *Mrs Noah and the Minoan Queen* (1984) Sisters, Melbourne, to the author.

Ania Walwicz: 'fantasm' and 'red sails' published in *Boat* (1989) Angus and Robertson, to the author.

Elizabeth Biff Ward: 'Flipping the Switch', to the author.

Terry Whitebeach: 'Premenstrual', to the author.
Lauren Williams: 'Erotica', previously published in *Power and Desire*, Vol. 1, No. 1, 1985.

Every effort has been made to trace copyright holders, but in a few cases this has proved impossible. The publishers would be interested to hear from any copyright holders not acknowledged here or acknowledged incorrectly.

The Glass Whittler   Stephanie Johnson

A young woman changes cities, but no one in the new city needs a glass whittler; Robyn, a single mother, buys a house on the proceeds of an unusual business; Nola is fat – one night reminded of the joys of chocolate by the television she decides to go out – but Nola is locked inside her flat and cannot get out; a retired schoolmistress who has had a stroke is cared for by an alcoholic tramp who has made himself at home in her flat.

Twelve stories by a remarkable young writer, Stephanie Johnson writes about craving for love and companionship, for security and the approval of others. The people in these stories seem to find unusual ways of coping with the absurdities and constraints of modern life. But perhaps their solutions are not so strange.

The Penguin Book of Australian Women Poets   Edited by Susan Hampton and Kate Llewellyn

This anthology represents eighty-nine Australian women poets, from tribal Aboriginal singers through to the present.

The range of subjects and styles is as wide as the differences in the lives of the poets. There are poems about the selector's wife and daughter, factory work, prostitutes, social conventions, feminism, lovers, Japan, old age, happy marriage, the conflict between love and independence, and the Sydney Harbour Bridge. There are poems that do not exist in official histories, as well as poems that have come to be regarded as classics.

The Penguin Book of Australian Women Poets presents for the first time an overview of the traditions, the voices and the range of women's poetry in Australia.

FOR THE BEST PAPERBACKS, LOOK FOR THE

PENGUIN

The Hanged Man in the Garden   Marion Halligan

'. . . the Hanged Man dangles gallantly by one foot and turning upside down observes the world. Its powers cannot harm him, he sees it clearly and afresh, all new. He is an individual. And he has a halo round his head.'

The Hanged Man represents a turn around of perception that often occurs when an individual confronts pain. A baby dies, a husband is unfaithful, a woman spends a week in a cupboard, people strive to come to terms with grief and loss – variously they choose humour, despair, irony and hope. It is the unexpectedness of this illogical reversal that makes the experience precious. And, how ever hard life may be, the sensuous beauty of its surfaces is a source of pleasure.

One of Australia's foremost short story writers, Marion Halligan explores, through the interweaving lives of a group of individuals, the complexities of pain.

West Block   Sara Dowse

Canberra's attendant lords look like settling down after a crisis that has rocked Australia.

In West Block, the flawed human world behind the headlines, George Harland consummates his career as a public servant; Henry Beeker prepares to fight for a policy; Catherine Duffy confronts the consequences of Australia's Vietnam policy; Jonathan Roe stumbles on happiness; and Cassie Armstrong's ironic intelligence leads her to despair.

But the whispers of a different past move through the rumbling hulk of a building which embodies the history of a capital city and has a future as uncertain as the nation it symbolizes.